A Matter of Trust

ANNE SCHRAFF

Series Editor: Paul Langan

SCHOLASTIC INC.

New York Toronto London Auckland Sydney
Mexico City New Delhi Hong Kong Buenos Aires

ISBN-13: 978-0-439-86547-0
ISBN-10: 0-439-86547-6

12 11 10 9 8 7 6 5 4   7 8 9 10 11 12/0

Printed in the U.S.A.   01

This edition first printing, January 2007

Chapter 1

Darcy Wills clenched her hands so hard that her fingernails dug into her palms. Hakeem Randall was walking to the front of the classroom to give his English report on *Macbeth*. He was a good student, but when he got nervous, he stuttered. Darcy dreaded this moment. She knew that if he began to stutter, the class would show no mercy. Just thinking about how embarrassed he would be made her cringe.

"Oh, Tarah," Darcy whispered to her friend, "I feel so *bad* for him!"

Tarah Carson turned a stern eye on Darcy, "Girl, he gotta fight this battle himself by doin' just what he's doin', facin' it."

Darcy had been dating Hakeem for just a few weeks, but at times it seemed that she had known him forever. He was a tall, handsome boy with a lot going for him—he was a good student, a great singer and guitar player, and a really nice person.

"My report on *Macbeth*," Hakeem began, "is about how g-g-guilt p-p-played an important p-p-part in the story." Darcy's worst fears were coming true. She had never heard him stutter so badly. A soft ripple of laughter began in the back row and spread around the room.

Mr. Keenan, the teacher, glared at the students. "Let's try to remember this is tenth grade English, not second grade recess!" he growled. It did not help much. Hakeem struggled on with his report, stuttering often. Stifled giggles erupted throughout the room, gurgling like an underground spring. Roylin Bailey was making a big show of covering his mouth with both hands while he rocked back and forth.

"T-t-tomorrow, and t-t-tomorrow, and t-t-tomorrow," Hakeem stammered, "creeps in this p-p-petty p-p-pace from day to day—"

"Is 't-t-tomorrow' the same thing as 'tomorrow,' Mr. Keenan?" Roylin asked cruelly. "'Cause I want to know, sir."

Tarah's boyfriend, Cooper Hodden, just shook his head while other kids laughed. Cringing, Tarah shrank down in her seat. This was as hard for Hakeem's friends to watch as it was for Hakeem to endure, Darcy thought. Then, finally, mercifully, Hakeem's report was over, and he fled to his desk like a soldier racing across a battlefield and diving into a safe ditch.

Darcy reached over and covered Hakeem's hand with hers, whispering, "It was a good report."

Hakeem pulled his hand away, anger flaring in his usually warm eyes. "I made a fool of myself," he said bitterly.

Through the rest of the class, Hakeem sat staring at his desk and fiddling so violently with his pencil that he broke it in two. Darcy knew he was reliving the humiliation of the report. He told her once that he would replay his stuttering spells over and over in his mind. His speech therapist said there was nothing really wrong with him—it was something he would eventually overcome. But not today.

When the bell rang, Darcy hurried after Hakeem. "Hakeem, it wasn't that bad, really it wasn't!" she assured him.

Hakeem slammed his fist into his open palm and shook his head. "It was stupid! I'm stupid! If I wasn't stupid, I could talk right!"

"Hey man," Cooper said, standing in front of the snack machines, "don't sweat it. We all feel stupid sometimes. Once, I gave an oral presentation, and people were laughing but I didn't know why. Then the teacher whispered to me that my fly was unzipped."

"Yeah, and he was wearin' bright red boxer shorts that day," Tarah chimed in, smirking.

Hakeem jammed change into the soda-machine slot. He yanked out the can and walked away without saying anything. When Darcy tried to follow him, Tarah grabbed her wrist. "Girl," Tarah scolded, "give it a rest. We all got our lumps and bumps, and nobody gets outta this world without bein' banged up. It's not the end of the world that Hakeem messed up on a report. Let him work it out his own self."

Darcy reluctantly let Hakeem walk down the corridor alone. She felt so bad for him. Right now he was hating himself, and she understood that. Darcy had hated herself all through middle school and her first year at Bluford High because boys just seemed to ignore her. Every other girl in her class seemed prettier, more popular, and Darcy's shyness hurt something like Hakeem's stutter must have.

Darcy walked slowly towards the library to work on a science report. Her father had offered to take her to the Palomar Observatory for the report. The observatory would have made a great topic, but Darcy turned him down. Her father had been away from the family for five years, and now he was trying to rebuild his relationship with them. But Darcy felt awkward and strange with him.

Now she felt estranged from Hakeem too. He was hurting so much, and he would not let her try to help.

As Darcy reached the library, she noticed a flyer posted on the door:

Talent show auditions.
February 20, Noon.
Singers, musicians, dancers, artists.

The depressing thoughts of a moment ago were suddenly forgotten. Darcy's heart raced with excitement over what this could mean for Hakeem.

Everyone knew he was a great guitar player and a wonderful singer. When he sang, he never stuttered. Darcy could not wait till school was over so she could track him down. This show was just what he needed to boost his spirits.

After school, Darcy found Hakeem sitting under the pepper tree behind the Bluford parking lot. His guitar was resting on his lap. She sat beside him on the grass and said, "Did you hear about the auditions for the talent show? You'd be just great for that, Hakeem. You'd blow 'em away!"

"Yeah, watch the stuttering idiot perform. Maybe I could do a ventriloquist act so the kids'll think the dummy is the one who stutters!" Hakeem said bitterly.

"But you don't stutter when you sing," Darcy pointed out.

"I guess," he said, rolling a red berry between his fingers and watching the papery skin pop off, leaving a little brown seed. "Why don't *you* audition, Darcy? You have a nice singing voice. And you don't stutter."

"Oh, I'm no singer," Darcy blushed.

"Sure you are," Hakeem insisted. "I've heard you. And you told me you

6

used to sing in a church choir."

"But that's because Mom made me."

"Well, you should really enter this contest. It might give you that spark to start singing again."

"I will if you will," Darcy said impulsively, though the very thought of performing before the student body made her shudder.

Hakeem finally smiled. "Okay. Deal. Maybe we'll both make such fools of ourselves we'll have to run away to a desert island and hide."

Darcy glanced at her watch. A neighbor, Ms. Harris, was sitting with Darcy's grandmother, but Darcy still had to be home soon. "Gotta go now," she said. "Grandma will be needing me."

"How is she?" Hakeem asked.

Darcy shrugged. Grandma hadn't been well since her stroke a year and a half ago. "She's about the same. Some days, she's, you know, almost like normal for a few hours, and then she's back to thinking she's a little girl in her mom's house. I think she always knows me. I mean, she calls me 'Angelcake,' and she's always got a smile for me."

"Your parents getting any closer?" Hakeem asked.

"Dad goes down to the hospital where Mom works, and sometimes they talk in the cafeteria. I don't know if Mom would ever let him come back or even if he wants to. He's just trying to make up for what happened, you know, for running out on us."

"You want your parents together again, Darcy?"

"I don't know. Dad gets along good with Jamee. Even when we were little, she was always closer to him than I was. Maybe it's because she's two years younger than me, and Dad was always ready to baby her. I think right now she's ready to forgive him, but I can't say I am ready to do that. Maybe I should, but it's hard," Darcy admitted.

Hakeem gave Darcy a quick hug. "Like Tarah is always saying, 'We gotta make the best of what we got 'cause there ain't nothin' else to do!'"

They both laughed, and Hakeem picked up his guitar. He strummed a melody and began to sing in his rich, deep voice:

Will you hear me if I cry,
Above the thunder of anger,
Over blasts of fear and hate,

When help comes not at all,
Or when it comes too late?
When streets explode with fire,
And hearts grow dead with grief,
When all the sounds are sad,
And there's no more relief?
Will you hear me if I cry?
Will you come before I die?

"Did you just write that?" Darcy asked.

"A couple of weeks ago. I was visiting my cousins, and we were talking about Russell Walker, that guy who went down in a drive-by shooting last year. I sort of wrote it for him."

"Yeah, I heard about him," Darcy said. "He was an honor student and an athlete, wasn't he?"

Hakeem nodded somberly.

"That was a crying shame," she added. "I hope they catch the guys who did it and put them behind bars for good."

Darcy was heading home when she ran into Brisana Meeks. Until just a few weeks ago, they had been best friends. When Darcy started hanging out with Tarah, Cooper and their friends, Brisana cut off the friendship. Since then, Darcy had made small efforts to repair their relationship. "Hey, Brisana," Darcy said, "how's it going?"

"Terrific," Brisana said with a sharp edge to her voice. Brisana had once told Darcy that she and Darcy were the bright, sophisticated kids at Bluford High. They were the "tens." It was their duty to avoid the low-class, stupid kids like Tarah and Cooper, who were zeroes.

"Want to go to the mall on Saturday, Brisana?" Darcy asked.

"With *you?*" Brisana scoffed, placing her hands on her hips. "No thanks," she added, leaving Darcy speechless.

As Darcy walked on, Roylin Bailey pulled up alongside her in a teal-blue Honda. "Hey Darcy, want a lift?" he shouted.

"No, thanks," Darcy said.

"Come on, Darcy," Roylin persisted. "Why are you wastin' your time with that stuttering fool? Sistah, I'm here to tell you, he ain't the one."

"Roylin, leave me alone. I don't remember asking for your opinion on my social life," Darcy snapped.

"Relax, girl. I'm just tryin' to help you out. You know, pass on the male perspective. And from where I'm sittin' you could do a lot better than Ha-ke-ke-ke-keem," he said, snickering.

Out of the corner of her eye, Darcy saw Cooper Hodden's beat-up truck roll up behind the Honda. Tarah, sitting beside Cooper, yelled, "Cooper, baby, you know your brakes ain't so good. Don't go smashin' that Honda now!"

"I can't stop!" Cooper howled, hitting the horn and blasting Roylin's Honda out of his path. Both Cooper and Tarah doubled over laughing as Roylin sped away.

"You guys are outta your minds!" Darcy said, also laughing. "Thanks, I owe you." Leaning in the truck window, she confided, "Hey, guess what. I told Hakeem I'd sign up for the talent show that's coming up, just to make him try out. Problem is, I'm terrified of getting up in front of all those people. And then there's the issue of my voice."

"What's wrong with your voice?" Cooper asked. "You talkin' okay right now."

"No, my *singing* voice. It doesn't exactly make people jump to their feet with applause. Fall to their knees begging me to stop, maybe, but not jump to their feet," Darcy said.

"Girl, don't even worry about it," Tarah advised. "Just play the music real loud, smile real pretty, and nobody'll notice how you sing."

"Thanks, I'll keep that in mind," Darcy replied sarcastically.

Darcy climbed into the cramped front seat of the pickup truck for a ride home just as Hakeem sped by on a shiny silver motorbike. Hakeem did not seem to notice Darcy, but she saw him— with Brisana Meeks sitting behind him with her arms around his waist.

"That's weird," Darcy said. "I haven't even seen his new bike, and there she is riding on it."

"He prob'ly just givin' her a lift," Tarah said.

"Don't know about that," Cooper chimed in. "That girl's *fine*."

Tarah nudged Cooper in the ribs with her elbow, and he howled. But the damage was done. It was done the minute Darcy saw Brisana riding on Hakeem's motorbike.

"Brisana always used to make fun of Hakeem because he stuttered," Darcy said.

"Stuck-up girl like her, she prob'ly just going after him to mess with your head," Tarah replied.

Or maybe, Darcy thought, *I like Hakeem a lot more than he likes me.* A cold chill pressed down on Darcy's chest like a heavy blanket of ice.

Chapter 2

The next day, Darcy was walking down the long hallway on her way to English class. Both Hakeem and Brisana were in the class, and Darcy had made up her mind not to mention seeing them riding together yesterday. Whatever Darcy said would make her look bad. Hakeem would see her as being jealous, and Brisana would be delighted that she was so upset.

"Hi, Darcy," Brisana sang out as she started to pass Darcy in the hallway. "Boy, was I ever wrong about Hakeem. He's so sweet! He just insisted on driving me home yesterday."

Fury surged in Darcy. It would not have been as bad if Brisana really liked Hakeem, but Darcy knew that wasn't true. She had seen Brisana make fun of his stuttering before. "I can't believe you, Brisana! You're so full of it!" Darcy cried.

Brisana took a step back. "Excuse me?" she snapped, crossing her arms on her chest.

"I know you're being fake with Hakeem," Darcy went on, unable to hold back her feelings.

"Fake?!"

"Yeah, a few days ago you were making fun of him, and now you're riding around on the back of his motorbike. I know you're only doing this to get back at me because I've become friends with Tarah and Cooper."

"Darcy," Brisana spoke in a mocking voice, "are you *jealous?*"

"Jealous!" Darcy exclaimed, her pulse pounding in her neck.

"It's obvious that you are," Brisana snapped. "And why wouldn't you be? You're the one who can't even hold on to the first boy who ever paid any attention to you. Besides, if all of a sudden you can find *sooo* much in common with losers like Tarah and Cooper, surely I can change my mind about Hakeem. Which reminds me, I've got to run. Hakeem's waiting for me in class." Brisana moved forward to walk down the hallway, but Darcy blocked her way. The next thing Darcy knew, Brisana stumbled and fell against a row of metal lockers, scraping her knee. A small cut began to bleed from just below her kneecap. Brisana staggered to her feet, crying, "Look what you did!"

"I didn't do anything!" Darcy snapped. "Can I help it if you're clumsy—trying to walk on those stupid mile-high heels!"

Darcy was shaking when she got to English. *I almost got into a fight with Brisana over a guy!* she thought. *What's wrong with me?*

Roylin Bailey's desk was two rows away from Hakeem's, and it was still two minutes before the beginning of class.

"P-p-pardon me, Hakeem, b-b-but what t-t-time is it?" Roylin asked Hakeem as he came in.

"Shut your stupid mouth, Roylin," Darcy demanded.

"Oh, are you Hakeem's mommy?" Roylin asked in a mocking voice. "I guess Hakeem needs a mommy, 'cause he stutters like a baby."

A wave of laughter rippled through the room as Mr. Keenan walked in. He glared at the students and said, "Levity is over and terror begins. A pop quiz." He whipped out a stack of papers from his tan briefcase. "Let's see if we can match the quotations to the persons who spoke them in *Macbeth*." The multiple-choice tests were quickly passed down the rows as Mr. Keenan warned, "Don't embarrass yourselves by copying from your neighbors, dear scholars, for there are different tests for each row."

Darcy had read *Macbeth* more than once, so she had no problem with the quiz, but several students, including Roylin, seemed to have trouble with the questions.

After class, Darcy and Hakeem walked out together. "Look, Darcy," Hakeem said, "I know you want to help, but don't stick up for me in class, okay? It just makes me look like even more of a fool than I already am. I mean, my mom used to do that. I'd be playing and I'd stutter, and the guys would diss me, and there'd be Mom yelling at them. I'd feel so bad I'd wish I was dead, and you know something? Sometimes I still do!"

Darcy felt shocked and hurt, as if she had been slapped in the face. "Don't talk like that!" Darcy cried. "It only makes things worse!"

"Will you just let me handle this on my own," Hakeem said, with an angry edge in his voice.

Darcy took a step back. She did not mean to upset Hakeem. She only wanted to help him. But it did not seem like Hakeem wanted her around. Maybe he would rather go to Brisana for comfort, Darcy thought bitterly.

"I'm sorry, Hakeem."

"It's okay. Forget it. Just forget it." Hakeem tried to smooth things over with a weak smile, but even his golden-brown eyes failed to warm. Darcy hurried to her next class and tried to concentrate on her astronomy project. She was writing a report on whether or not human beings would ever be able to colonize Mars. It seemed stupid to even think about it. Darcy forced herself to do her outline about a man-made plastic roof stretching over areas of the planet that would allow human beings to live. When tears ran down her cheeks, she dragged her sleeve across her face and went on working.

After her last class, Darcy hurried past the Asian grocery store as a slender woman carefully laid out a tray of chicken. *I know why she's alone,* Darcy thought bitterly to herself. *She's probably got a husband who left her to raise her children and pay the bills.* As she watched the woman work, Darcy imagined the struggle her own mother faced when her father left. She fought each day to hold a job, a home, and a family together with no help. All the while, Darcy thought, her father was living with another woman in New York City. Darcy studied the Asian woman carefully. She did not know anything about her, of course. Maybe her husband was a loyal, hard-working man. Darcy did not know. But right now all Darcy could think of was that men, and boys, were heartless beings.

Often when Darcy returned from school, she was the first one home. Then Mom would go racing off to her job as an emergency-room nurse. But today Eleanor Harris, a neighbor, was sitting with Grandma.

"Grandma wasn't any trouble, was she?" Darcy asked.

"Oh, no trouble at all. She was a perfect little lamb," Ms. Harris assured her. "As a matter of fact, she's sleeping now. She had a nice fruit cocktail and some of her nutrition drink not too long ago." Picking up her handbag, Ms. Harris prepared to leave. "Well, I'm gonna run now. Tell your mom I'll talk to her tomorrow."

"Sure thing. And thanks, Ms. Harris,"

Darcy said as she shut the door behind her kind neighbor.

Soon after Ms. Harris left, Jamee burst in from school. Only a month ago, she was getting terrible grades and hanging out with a bad crowd. But when Dad reappeared, she seemed to change for the better. She still played rap music much too loud, and Mom had to stop her from wearing short skirts to school, but she was getting decent grades now. And she had gotten rid of Bobby Wallace, the boyfriend who once punched her in an argument. Now she was dating a kid named Tyrone Penn whose worst fault was wearing a ton of gold chains.

"I got a B in math, Darcy," Jamee announced.

Darcy gave her sister a big hug. "That's great, Jamee. I'm so proud of you!"

Jamee wriggled free of the embrace. "And guess what! Tyrone is going with me to the school dance, and he called me his girl! And you know what else? I'm going out to dinner with Daddy and we're eating at a fancy restaurant."

Darcy felt a cold chill pass through her heart. She was not as willing to forgive and forget everything their father had done. He had neglected his family for five long years and was just barely back, and Jamee was already holding her arms open as if he was some returning hero. "When did you decide to go to dinner with Dad?" Darcy asked coldly.

"Well, you know he's been asking both of us. You know that. I mean, don't get all bent out of shape or nothing. He's asked both of us like a hundred times," Jamee said, dropping onto the sofa.

"He hasn't been home long enough to do *anything* a hundred times," Darcy replied sharply. "I mean, he just blew in from New York, right?"

"What's the matter with you, Darcy?" Jamee groaned. "Are you jealous or something? Are you mad that I'm getting a little time with Dad?" Jamee demanded, her eyes flashing.

"It's just that you don't seem to care what he did to Mom, or us. All of a sudden he's some hero," Darcy said, her voice trembling.

"So what do you *want*, Darcy?" Jamee almost screamed. "Maybe Dad should be thrown in prison. I mean, you're always talking about love and forgiveness and all that stuff, and now you want us to hate Dad forever and ever!"

Darcy began to cry. "Jamee, I'm

sorry. It's just that he hurt us all so bad—"

"I don't care," Jamee said defiantly. "I just want my father back. I'm going to dinner with him, and if you don't like it, too bad. Mom says it's okay, and I'm going! That's all there is to it!" Jamee got up and stomped off to her room. A second later, Darcy heard her sister's bedroom door slam. The yelling and fighting reminded Darcy of how things were just before Jamee ran away from home. Though it had been over a month since that night, Darcy remembered it as if it was yesterday. And now, with Jamee's sudden outburst, it seemed as if that painful time had not even passed. Loud rap music throbbed through the walls of Jamee's room.

> *What's goin' down, what's comin'*
>   *down,*
> *The bad you done is comin' back*
>   *aroun'.*
> *You can try to hide,*
> *You can say you tried,*
> *Word on the street,*
> *Somebody died.*

Darcy went to her grandmother's room and sat down beside her bed. Grandma was sleeping fitfully. Her Bible was on the nightstand at her side. Grandma could not see well enough to read it, and she no longer understood much of what was read to her, but she still liked hearing the familiar words. Darcy picked up the old Bible. It had originally belonged to Darcy's great-grandparents.

"To our beloved daughter, Annie Louella Duncan," read the beautifully written inscription on the first page, "on her wedding day." Then, in Grandma's careful handwriting, were recorded the births of her four children, the births of grandchildren, the death of Emmit Duncan, her husband, and the death of her firstborn son on a foreign battlefield in some war she had now forgotten.

Grandma stirred, her eyes sliding open. "Mama?" she called out in a puzzled, plaintive voice.

"I'm here, Grandma. It's Darcy," Darcy said, taking Grandma's hand.

"My Mama was here," Grandma said, smiling. "She was just here. She read me some nice stories from the Bible. You should have been here. She read me about Joseph's coat of many colors."

"I'm glad," Darcy said. Grandma, in her confusion, was probably mistaking Ms. Harris, their neighbor, for her own mother.

"Mama sang to me—she sang 'Deep River,' you know, that hymn I like so much."

"Yes, Grandma," Darcy said. "It's a lovely song."

Grandma drifted off to sleep then, and Darcy gently put the frail woman's hand down on the blanket. Darcy went to her room and began looking through her music collection. She had to practice for the audition she had foolishly committed to, just to help Hakeem. Darcy did not want to make a complete fool of herself. She came across a song she had not heard in years and began to sing softly.

Dream on baby,
You will be his lady,
In his eyes you'll see his smile,
At least for a little while.
Dream on baby,
And hope the night is long,
And pray that you'll be strong,
When he's gone.

Just then, the phone rang. Darcy picked it up.

"Darcy, I'm sorry I've been acting like a jerk," Hakeem said.

"Oh, hello, Hakeem."

"There's been so much stuff going on. I'm in a track meet on Saturday. I really need to make a good showing for my Dad. He just finished chemo, and he needs something to cheer him up, like me sprinting first over the finish line on Saturday. So could you come? And then we could—"

"I didn't know your dad was having chemotherapy."

"Yeah, well, he's okay about it. But he needs a distraction, you know. He's a real sports nut. S-s-so, you think you could come, Darcy?" Hakeem sounded nervous.

"Sure," Darcy said.

"Great," Hakeem said before he hung up. "I'll save you a seat."

The brief conversation with Hakeem was enough to lift Darcy's spirits. After she rehearsed the song a few more times, she went to the kitchen and put a pair of frozen dinners in the microwave.

"Yum, yum, just like Grandma used to make," Jamee said, sitting at the kitchen table and scribbling on a page of her history notebook.

"Okay, so homemade is better, but I'd rather have this stuff than nothing," Darcy said, glancing at Jamee stabbing the notebook paper with the point of a freshly sharpened pencil. "You've got a report due on Andrew Jackson, don't you? You better get started."

Jamee made a face. "Like it matters to me what this guy did two hundred years ago. Hey, know what, Darcy? Wouldn't it be cool if you could get to a real good place in your life and then just stop? I mean not to go on to the next bad thing. Tyrone is being so *nice* to me I can't believe it. I wish we could stay like we are right now, just having fun."

Darcy checked on the dinners in the microwave. "Just don't let him start making you do what you don't want to do."

"Does Hakeem push you to do stuff you don't want to do?" Jamee asked.

"No," Darcy said.

"I think Hakeem's cool," Jamee said. "But Amberlynn says he's retarded."

"Retarded?" Darcy snapped. "That's the most stupid thing I ever heard of. What does some eighth grader know about Hakeem anyway?"

"Amberlynn's brother, Roylin Bailey,

goes to Bluford, and he's in classes with Hakeem. Roylin told Amberlynn that Hakeem stutters like somebody who's retarded, and everybody laughs at him," Jamee said.

"Roylin Bailey is a fool. You ever see the way he drools at girls? That boy needs to wipe his chin or wear a bib or something!" Darcy fumed.

Jamee burst into a fit of laughter, knocking her notebook off the small table.

But Darcy felt wounded. People teased Hakeem because of his stuttering problem. Yet everybody in this neighborhood had so many problems, Darcy thought, so why try to drag Hakeem down for his speech problem? He was a good student and a pretty good athlete. He could sing better than anyone else she knew. And he had a heart of gold. No one, she thought, had any right to make fun of him for anything. No one.

Chapter 3

"Darcy," Jamee said, picking at her dinner, "how do you know if a person is . . . you know . . . being honest?"

"You kinda don't for a long time, I guess, and then maybe—" Darcy said.

"You think Dad's gonna hurt us again, don't you?" Jamee interrupted, looking right at Darcy.

"I really don't know, Jamee, but be real. He *did* run out on us."

"I know he left us," Jamee said, her eyes suddenly narrowing, "but I feel good when I'm with him. He says I'm pretty and special and stuff. Mom's always nagging at me, and I know she loves me and all that, but it's like she's always reminding me of everything I do wrong. It's like Dad thinks I'm perfect, you know?"

Darcy was sitting on the sofa reading when her mother came home near midnight. "You still up, sweetie? Tomorrow's a school day, you know."

"I took a nap, Mom. Boy, do you look tired."

"I am *exhausted!*" Mom said, collapsing into her recliner. "Baby, it was pure hell in the ER tonight. Man came in with full cardiac arrest, and we couldn't get ahold of his regular doctor, and this other doctor did the wrong procedure, and now we're all in hot water. This doctor comes in yelling and cussing and saying somebody is going to be fired. Then we get a little girl with a real bad asthma attack and a boy with a knife in his back, and in the middle of all that, this same doctor is losing it. I'm telling you, I had to talk tough to that doctor, and he looked like he was going to have a heart attack right there in the ER! He was thinking to himself, 'Who is this nurse talking to me like this? Who does she think she is, speaking to a doctor this way?' It took him a while, but he finally calmed down. It must've been the first time a nurse ever addressed him like that."

"Oh, Mom, I wish you didn't have such a hard job," Darcy said.

"Well, your father is helping me with money now. He's doing real well at that men's clothing store. You know how charming he can be when he wants to be. He's selling five-hundred-dollar suits like ice cream in July."

"So maybe you could quit working so hard," Darcy suggested.

"Oh no, sweetie. I won't ever quit my job. With all the downsizing going on, maybe there won't be any choice. Maybe one day something like tonight will happen, and they'll write me up and fire me. But as long as I can keep that job, I will. I can't depend on your father. I can't put our lives in the hands of a man who walked out once before."

"You don't think he's changed, Mom?" Darcy asked.

"Oh my Lord, I don't know," Mom sighed. "Maybe he has. Maybe he hasn't. I just don't trust him. Maybe I ought to, but I just don't. If he ran off once, what's to stop him from doing it again?" Mom got up slowly from the recliner, rubbing the small of her back with her hand. "Trust, honey. Such an itty-bitty word, five little letters strung together. I trusted my Daddy. My Mama, she trusted Daddy. If he were here today, he'd be standing by your Grandma. Now that was a man who was a straight arrow. Trust, oh baby, there's a world of pain when it's gone."

Darcy ran into Tarah on her way to school the next day. Tarah was entering some sketches in the art section of the talent show. "Tarah, I can't believe I ever agreed to audition for the talent show. I'm scared just thinking about it," Darcy said.

"Girl, you got guts," Tarah laughed. "Not that you ain't got a nice little voice, but standing up there in front of everybody'd give me the hives!"

"It gives me the hives too. But Hakeem needed a push to audition. He's so good, Tarah. You know that. Maybe if he wins, he'll feel good about himself."

"Darcy, I can hate myself and love myself different times *every* day! I look in the mirror and I say, 'Hey, is that the biggest, roundest chocolate pie I ever saw, or is that my fat face?' Then I get to laughin' over something my little brother did, and I catch my smile in the lookin' glass, and I'm saying 'Whoa, girl, you got a smile that's gonna light up the world, least your little part of it,' and then I'm fine."

Darcy laughed. "I tried to sing last night, and I sounded like a squeaking door," she said.

Chuckling, Tarah said, "I told you, girl, just play the music real loud, and you'll be fine."

On Saturday, Darcy went to the track meet with Tarah and Cooper. On the ride over, all Darcy could think about was Brisana. Would she show up too? That would spoil everything. "I can just see her dancing around Hakeem," Darcy grumbled. "Just rubbing it in my face."

"Just be cool, girl," Tarah said. "If Hakeem falls for that game, then he's a loser, and you ought to blow him off."

"Man, how come he rates?" Cooper said enviously. "That boy's got two girls fightin' over him. I sure wouldn't mind two honeys fightin' over me, I'll tell you that."

"Don't even go there, Cooper," Tarah warned. "After I got through with her, I'd come after you!"

Friends and supporters of both track teams filled the bleachers under a brilliant sun. Darcy and her friends headed for the Bluford High cheering section.

Hakeem spotted Darcy and introduced her to his parents.

"Nice to meet you, Darcy," Hakeem's father said with a warm smile. He was wearing a baseball cap to cover the hair loss from the chemotherapy, but he looked good.

As the track meet got underway, Hakeem's father told Darcy, "I used to compete in field events in high school. I wasn't as good as my boy, though. He's a born athlete."

Darcy began to relax. It looked as if Brisana was not coming, and that was a big relief. Darcy was eager to hang out with Hakeem alone after the meet.

The boys were at the starting blocks for the 400-meter dash. Darcy kept her eyes fixed on Hakeem as he sprang into motion. It soon became a duel between Hakeem and a lanky boy from Lincoln High School. He was taller than Hakeem and had the raw power Darcy had seen in famous sprinters on TV.

"Come on, boy, you can do it," Mr. Randall was shouting, his face animated with excitement. Darcy could see that it was so important for Hakeem to win this race for his dad. As the runners turned the final corner and headed for the straightaway, Hakeem had a narrow lead. Mr. Randall was on his feet, clapping and cheering. But the boy from Lincoln started edging ahead. He passed Hakeem and flew across the finish line. Mr. Randall looked sad for a moment. Then he smiled and said, "Hey, it was a great race, and he almost won, didn't he?"

Darcy watched Hakeem give his father the second-place trophy. Both parents hugged a smiling Hakeem, but there was something in his eyes that seemed to contradict his smile.

As Darcy and Hakeem rode out of the parking lot on his motorbike, Hakeem said, "I don't like sports. I just do it for my dad. He's always been after me to get into sports—track, football, basketball. I've got three sisters, so I'm the only hope for him to have an athlete son. All his h-h-hopes for reliving his glory days in s-s-sports rest on me."

Darcy had rarely heard Hakeem stutter when he was not in front of a crowd. Now, while they were alone together, just thinking about his father's expectations was making him stutter. "You looked great out there," she said, tightening her arms around his waist.

"I always hated competition," he admitted. "I'd shoot baskets with the guys, but I s-s-stayed away from joining the school team or anything. Then Dad got s-sick. You know, I felt guilty, like I'd cheated him out of all those years he wanted to watch me play. I got s-scared. What if he didn't get well? Then he'd never g-g-get to see me do sports. So I got into this track thing. Well, second is okay, I guess. It sure beats nothing, huh?" There was a rich vein of sadness in Hakeem's voice.

They stopped at Niko's, a small pizza place that looked shabby but had the best pizza in town. After ordering pepperoni pizza and sodas, they sat down.

"So, how's it going with you, Darcy?" Hakeem asked. He seemed eager to change the subject from his own problems. "Are you getting to know your dad since he came back?"

"Not really. My sister Jamee is with him today. They got a big day planned. She acts like he never left. She's been so lonely for Dad. But I haven't seen him much. We've talked on the phone, but I feel weird with him. I mean, when he helped us find Jamee when she ran away and got lost, I was really grateful, but . . ." Darcy shook her head sadly.

"You should try to make up, Darcy. Just get together over hamburgers or something. Don't let it go. Like with my Dad, he's a great guy, but we had a lot of big fights. He thinks my music is stupid, and I hated how he tried to push me into sports. We both said lousy things to each other. I told him I hated him. And then when he got cancer, it hit me like a ton of bricks. My Dad had something bad, and maybe he wouldn't always be around, and we were wasting time fighting over something stupid."

Darcy took another slice of pizza. "Yeah, but Hakeem, your dad was there for you, big fights or not. My dad just left. No goodbye, no cards, no nothing. He can't expect to waltz back in and have everybody falling over themselves for him."

"I know, Darcy, and I'm not saying you're wrong. All I'm saying is maybe you could give your dad a second chance. From where I'm sitting, it looks like he's trying awful hard."

"You've got a point," Darcy conceded. "I'll think about it."

Hakeem pulled his motorbike to a stop in front of Darcy's house. For several seconds he hugged her, and Darcy gave him a soft kiss on his lips.

"Thanks for everything," she said.

Hakeem smiled. "I'll call you," he said, starting the engine of his motor-bike. Then he drove away slowly, the drone of the bike's engine fading into the distance.

"Did you have a good time, sweetie?" Mom asked.

"Yeah," Darcy said.

"Good. You didn't forget tomorrow, did you?"

"What's tomorrow?" Darcy asked, concerned.

"We have to go have dinner with Aunt Charlotte. Ms. Harris will be staying with Mama."

"Oh, Mom!" Darcy whined, plopping down onto the sofa.

"Don't you 'oh Mom' me. She's my only sister. I know she can be a pain, but she's still family," Mom scolded.

"Is Jamee going?"

"Of course. I've given her strict orders to dress nicely and behave like a lady. Last time we were over there, I about died of shame because of the way that child acted. But I had a talk with Jamee. If she wants to go anywhere this week—with your father or her friends—she'll treat Aunt Charlotte politely."

"Is Jamee still out with Dad?" Darcy asked.

"Yeah. They're making a day of it."

Darcy went to Grandma's room and helped her to the bathroom. Then she fed Grandma some rice pudding. The elderly woman was very listless, and the whole meal was a struggle. She kept asking the same questions over and over, and when Darcy answered her, she asked the question still again. Was Grandma getting worse? Had the final decline begun? Or would she brighten again, and be sort of normal, and call Darcy "Angelcake" again?

"I love you, Grandma," Darcy said anxiously.

"Is it still raining?" Grandma asked.

"No, it isn't raining anymore," Darcy answered.

"Is it still raining?" Grandma asked again in a flat, weak voice.

"It will stop soon," Darcy said, her eyes brimming with tears. She knew that someday, maybe soon, Grandma would leave them. But Darcy could not stand thinking about that day. She kept hoping for a little more time, a few more twinkling smiles from Grandma, another chance to hear her talk about being a child picking blackberries in the summer.

All the way to Aunt Charlotte's townhouse, Jamee spoke about her dinner with Dad. "It was a really cool restaurant. The waiters were guys, and they were always asking us if we wanted more bread or something. I felt like some rich kid!" Jamee beamed. But as they neared Aunt Charlotte's townhouse, Jamee's mood darkened.

"Hello, Mattie, girls," Aunt Charlotte chirped when she met them at the door. Aunt Charlotte was Mom's sister, but she could have been her daughter. Aunt Charlotte had perfect, smooth skin like a girl. She bought expensive makeup, and her cocoa-butter complexion was dramatically highlighted by a rich blush on her cheeks. "I'm so glad to see you. I have something really important to talk about," Aunt Charlotte said, looking right at Darcy. "It concerns all of us as a family, but it particularly concerns you, Darcy."

Darcy felt like a butterfly stuck by a pin to a display. She did not want to be the topic of Aunt Charlotte's discussion. It was true that her aunt was one of the most beautiful women Darcy had ever seen. It was also true that she bought the nicest furniture for her townhouse and that she decorated the walls with expensive, fancy paintings. But despite everything, Darcy did not admire Aunt Charlotte, and she did not want to be like her. Even though they had arrived only minutes earlier, Darcy wished the dinner was already over.

Darcy would have rather been home in their small apartment with the spots on the wall where it had leaked during last winter's rains, where there was a cracked tile right in the middle of the kitchen floor, where the only art was the paint-by-numbers pictures that Grandma did years ago. Darcy reluctantly sat down at Aunt Charlotte's fancy table, dreading the conversation to come.

Chapter 4

Everyone was careful to praise Aunt Charlotte's newest cooking creation, a strange veal and broccoli dish with an odd, woody taste. Then they all went into the living room for coffee and cake. Darcy was relieved to see the cake was from a bakery. That meant Aunt Charlotte had not baked it.

"I'm concerned about the effect Mother's condition is having on your family, Mattie, especially on Darcy," Aunt Charlotte began.

"Charlotte, what are you talking about?" Mom responded. Darcy could tell by her voice that she, too, was worried about what Charlotte had to say.

"Mattie, I don't think having Mother at home is good for the girls, especially for Darcy," Aunt Charlotte went on. "It can't be easy on her or Jamee to have a working mother who's not around enough. It just doesn't seem fair that you are putting such a burden on your children."

"But we're fine with Grandma," Darcy broke in quickly. "We have a nice neighbor who helps out when we need her, and everyone is doing fine. Grandma doesn't bother us, not at all."

"Yeah," Jamee chimed in. "I'm helping more with Grandma now too. We work together most days."

Aunt Charlotte cast a pitying glance at the girls, as if Darcy and Jamee were toddlers whose opinions did not count. "It's all very noble and everything, Mattie. Your girls have good hearts, but it can't be healthy for them to have a sick old woman there twenty-four hours a day."

"Charlotte, I don't know what has gotten into you, but Darcy and Jamee are fine. Mom is not that much trouble, and even if she was, what right do you have telling me how I should be running my own house? You haven't volunteered to help with Mom." Darcy could hear the anger and tightness in her mother's voice.

Aunt Charlotte was unmoved. "I'm your sister, Mattie. If you are making a mistake, I'm going to tell you. Right now, your girls are not being given the attention and the time they deserve. You have to work extra hours just to support Mother. And while you are out, the girls are forced to be baby-sitters and nurses because you want to keep Mother in your home. It's not fair to keep Mother so close to you." Charlotte paused for a moment to look at everyone. For a second, Darcy thought her aunt sounded like a jealous young child. "Mother should be in a nursing home," Charlotte continued. "She has no personal assets, so the state would pay for her care. It wouldn't be a burden on either of us. This way your girls will be free to grow up without having to worry about her all the time."

Darcy could see that Aunt Charlotte's words hurt Mom. She knew that Mom often felt guilty for asking Darcy and Jamee to look after Grandma. In fact, a few months ago her mother had even asked Darcy if taking care of Grandma was too much for her. Darcy assured her not to worry, but she could see by the sad look in her mother's eyes that Charlotte's words made the feeling come back. Darcy wanted to tell Aunt

Charlotte that she was the meanest woman she ever met, that she would rather take care of Grandma than be the selfish woman that her aunt had become. But instead Darcy said, "Aunt Charlotte, we love Grandma. We don't want to send her away to some nursing home where she wouldn't know anybody."

"Oh, come on," Aunt Charlotte scoffed. "She doesn't know anyone now. She's senile."

"She does too know us," Jamee piped up. "Sometimes anyway. She calls us by name when she's having a good day. I mean, if she was all alone among strangers, she'd call our names and nobody would come."

Aunt Charlotte turned to her sister again. "Mattie, you're the adult in this situation. You can't let your kids make up your mind for you. Mother has lived her life, and there's no reason she can't be cared for adequately in a nursing home. She might even be happier there in her more lucid moments. I understand they have special activities for people like her—"

"Charlotte, this is our *mother* you're talking about! Why are you talking about her like she is some *thing*?" Mom yelled, tears welling in her eyes.

"Mattie, you're a nurse. You know how hard it is to care for people. Darcy and Jamee should not have to take care of Mother, keep her clean, feed her. Your children deserve more." Charlotte's words seemed carefully selected to hurt her mother's feelings, Darcy thought. Charlotte leaned forward and took a deep breath, as if she was preparing for a major announcement. "Which brings me to the real reason I need to talk to you all. This summer, I will be vacationing in France for a month, and I would be delighted to have you along, Darcy. I think it would be the experience of your life. It would help you see there's more to life than Bluford High School, your grandmother, and your rundown neighborhood."

Darcy was shocked. "France?" she gasped. The farthest from her home she ever was before was San Francisco, only a few hundred miles away.

Aunt Charlotte started to smile, wrinkling the perfect skin around her eyes. It was like watching a mask crumble a little. "Yes! France! Doesn't it just thrill you? The French Riviera, *chateaus*,

45

seeing Paris, and climbing the Eiffel Tower!"

"It's really great for you to ask me," Darcy stammered.

Aunt Charlotte turned to Jamee. "And don't you feel bad, Jamee. I will be asking you too when you are sixteen years old and learn to show some respect."

"I'd never go to France with you, Aunt Charlotte," Jamee said angrily, "Never!"

"Jamee, don't you talk to your aunt like that!" Mom warned.

"We'll see how you feel later, Jamee," Charlotte purred. "After Darcy comes home with stories of places you can't even dream of, you'll change your mind. So, Mattie, if you could get Mother settled in the nursing home during the next few months, Darcy and I could be ready to leave by the beginning of summer."

"Aunt Charlotte," Darcy said quickly, "thanks a lot for asking me, but I don't want to go."

"You mean because of the burdens of home?" Aunt Charlotte demanded.

Mom broke in, "Darcy, if you really want to go, we could get a home health care nurse for Mama. You could go on the trip."

"No, I really don't want to go," Darcy repeated.

Aunt Charlotte glared at Mom. "You see, Mattie? Do you see how this life has affected your daughter? Now she doesn't even want to take the opportunity of a lifetime. How much longer can you sacrifice your children by turning your home into a hospital?"

"That's enough, Charlotte!" Mom said with fury in her voice.

"Don't talk about Grandma like that!" Jamee yelled. "Man, I'm never coming back to this place!"

Aunt Charlotte gave Jamee an icy look. "I'm sorry to say, young lady, I doubt very much you'll ever get an invitation from me to go to Europe." She turned to Darcy then. "You don't have to decide right away. Just think about it."

Mom stood up to leave. Darcy quietly followed her. She was eager to get out of the townhouse and her aunt's presence. "I will. Thank you, Aunt Charlotte. It was really nice of you to ask me on the trip."

When Darcy, Jamee, and their mother were on their way home, Mom said, "Darcy, you know that would be a wonderful opportunity for you—"

"I'm not going," Darcy said flatly.

"I know Charlotte seems cold and heartless sometimes," Mom said, "but I hope I haven't been putting the burden of Mama on you girls too much. That wouldn't be fair."

"No!" Jamee cried. "I want to take care of Grandma."

"Me too," Darcy said. "When we were little, she was always there for us."

Mom stopped for a red light, then glanced at her daughters. "But it can't be easy having to rush home from school every day."

"Mom," Darcy groaned, "aren't you always telling us that life isn't supposed to be easy? I mean, aren't you always saying hard stuff is what makes us grow? Haven't you said that a thousand times?"

Mom smiled. "I guess that's the trouble with telling your kids stuff. Sometimes they remember it and toss it back at you. But just remember this, Darcy. If you want to take that trip this summer, you can get it done without Grandma going away. We'll find a way to take care of Grandma."

"I know," Darcy said, "but Mom, I wouldn't enjoy going on a trip with Aunt Charlotte."

Later, when they were almost home, Darcy asked her mother, "We'll never put Grandma in a nursing home, will we? I mean, that'd be like sending her away because we don't love her anymore."

"Baby," Mom said heavily, "I don't want to do that, but you know it could happen. If she got so sick that we couldn't take care of her anymore, what choice would we have?"

Darcy closed her eyes, her throat tightening. She remembered last summer when she used to volunteer a few days a week at a nursing home. The patients sat in wheelchairs or moved slowly in walkers. They seemed to always be searching for familiar faces. A frail old lady had asked Darcy if she had seen her daughter. "My daughter is coming today to take me home," she had said in a trembling voice. The nurse's aide had smiled and whispered to Darcy that the daughter lived in another state and would certainly never take her mother home. Other elderly people had called out names of people they half-remembered. Darcy could not bear for Grandma to be in such a place, calling in vain for her loved ones.

It would be like in that song Hakeem wrote,

Will you hear me if I cry?
Will you come before I die?

When they got home, Darcy went straight to Grandma's room. She found her sitting in a chair by the window. Ms. Harris was next to her and smiled when Darcy came in.

"I'm home, Grandma. Are you hungry?" Darcy asked.

"Your grandmother just finished her dinner," Ms. Harris said as she got up to leave. "She's been talking about you all night, Darcy. She calls you Angelcake."

Darcy thanked Ms. Harris before she left and then sat down next to her grandmother. "I love you, Grandma," she said.

Grandma smiled and then said, "I think I'll make a nice picnic basket and we can go to the mountains on Sunday. We went to the mountains last Sunday, and we had a nice time, didn't we? Carl was so funny. He was telling stories, don't you know. Your Daddy can be such a funny one," Grandma said.

"Yes, Grandma," Darcy said, taking Grandma's tiny, veined hand and pressing it to her cheek.

Tarah Carson was turning sixteen on the following Saturday, and she decided to invite all her friends to a party at a nearby bayfront park. "We can roast hot dogs, and my mom said she'll make her famous potato salad and even fry up some chicken. We'll throw on some CD's, Hakeem can play his guitar and sing— it'll be great!" Tarah declared.

"Yeah," Darcy agreed, "sounds like it'll be loads of fun. Hey, you're not inviting Brisana, are you?"

"Girl, I'm nice, but I ain't no fool. This party is for my *friends*, remember? Last I checked, Brisana don't fall nowhere near that category."

Darcy looked more closely at Tarah. She could not be sure, but it looked like Tarah had lost weight. "Tarah, you dieting or something? You look thinner."

A big smile spread over Tarah's face. "Girl, don't you bother givin' me no birthday present, you hear what I'm sayin'? You just gave me the best present a girl could get. I lost five pounds, and I didn't think anybody would notice! You better believe I been passin' up fries and chips and everything else that's good!"

All week, Tarah invited people to her party. She asked two dozen kids from her classes, a few of her cousins, and friends from the neighborhood youth center. It looked as if it was going to be a good mix of girls and boys. Everything went well until Wednesday, when Shanetta Greene confronted Tarah during Phys Ed. "Hey girl," she said, "how come you ain't invited nobody from 43rd Street to your party?"

"Got nothin' to do with no street," Tarah snapped. "We don't want trouble, you hear what I'm sayin'? It's gonna be a nice party with good food and good music, no fightin', no booze, you get my meanin'?"

Shanetta glared at Tarah. "Girl, I don't know what you talkin' about. You must be crazy or something."

"I seen you with Londell James and Bobby Wallace, Shanetta—you the one must be crazy, messin' with them," Tarah said. "They ain't nothin' but trouble."

"Girl, you need to get your eyes checked," Shanetta said. "I ain't hung around with them for months."

"Well, ain't that somethin'?" Tarah laughed. "I seen Londell's twin brother with you at the dollar store last night, and that's real strange 'cause he ain't got no twin brother!"

Shanetta rolled her eyes, turned, and stomped off.

"Londell James stole money out of my purse in middle school," Darcy said. "We were all scared of him."

"You told on him, didn't you?" Tarah asked.

"No," Darcy admitted. "Like I said, we were scared."

"That boy is real trouble."

"I know," Darcy said.

"Word on the street is that he's hangin' out with a bad bunch—and they got guns," Tarah said grimly.

After English class, Darcy spotted Roylin Bailey standing in front of the door to the library. He often loitered there so he could tease other kids. Lately Hakeem was his favorite target.

The two girls walked in Roylin's direction, and the boy immediately put on a mocking smile. "H-H-Hakeem here yet?" he asked.

"Boy, can't you find something better to do than make a fool of yourself?" Darcy snapped.

"I'm coming to the party Saturday," Roylin announced.

"You ain't invited," Tarah retorted.

"It's a public place," Roylin challenged. "You can't keep me away."

"You won't get nothin' to eat, boy, so you might as well stay at home," Tarah said.

"B-b-but I can spoil your party, can't I?" Roylin laughed.

Darcy and Tarah had not seen Hakeem walk up until he confronted Roylin. "Listen up, man, you get in my face, and I'm gonna change the way your face is arranged, you hear me?"

"You don't scare me, retard," Roylin said.

Hakeem took a step towards Roylin, his arms swinging. Darcy had never seen so much rage in his face.

"Here comes Keenan!" somebody yelled.

The tall teacher came around the corner carrying his briefcase. "The bell for the next class has rung. All you tough guys can either get in the classroom and sit down or go to the office," Mr. Keenan barked.

Chapter 5

The bayfront park had picnic tables under the trees and a small pier for fishing. There were at least a dozen barbecue pits and a clear area to fly kites. A cool wind was blowing, and the sky was bright blue. Darcy could smell the roasting chicken and hot dogs as she approached the parking lot. She spotted Tarah's party by the bunch of colorful balloons tied to a tree. Darcy hurried to add her gift, some art supplies, to those piled on a picnic table.

"Happy birthday, girl!" Darcy said as soon as she spotted Tarah. Both girls hugged briefly, but then Tarah turned away.

"I'll be right back, Darcy. I gotta watch Coop with the grill, or he'll burn all the food. Lord knows that boy can't cook!"

Darcy chuckled as Tarah went over to the grill. Hakeem was standing near-by holding his guitar. Just seeing it made Darcy anxious.

"I'm so nervous about the talent show," she said as he walked over to her. "I get butterflies just thinking about it."

"You'll be fine, Darcy," Hakeem replied. He seemed to be in a good mood.

"Man, I'm starvin'," Cooper complained. "These hot dogs are takin' forever!"

"They'll be done in a minute, Coop," Tarah said. "You don't wanna eat them raw, do you?"

"I gotta eat now," Cooper insisted playfully. "I'm a growin' boy."

"Where is the mustard?" Sonia asked. "Who was supposed to bring the mustard?"

"Nobody wants hot dogs without mustard," Cooper bellowed. Then he quickly said, "Hey, my man Shariff brought the mustard. Here it is."

"Tarah said for me to bring the con-tinents," Shariff said with a broad smile. "And I did."

"Not *continents*," Keisha explained gently, "*condiments*."

"Speakin' of continents, I'm hungry enough to eat a whole continent right now," Cooper said.

After Tarah opened her gifts, everybody began eating. Cooper wolfed down three hot dogs, and he still had appetite left for two slices of Tarah's chocolate birthday cake. Then some guys started a game of basketball. Some of the girls decided to watch. Others gathered in small groups, listened to music and talked about school and the latest gossip.

Hakeem and Darcy sat under a tree, and he strummed the strings on his guitar.

"I sound like a sick cat when I sing that stupid song I've been practicing. That singer on the CD makes it sound so good, but . . ."

"Sing some old classic," Hakeem suggested. "I got a great CD we can listen to. There's one song . . ."

Hakeem stopped talking and looked off in the distance. Darcy turned to see what he was looking at. A teal-blue Honda had just pulled into the parking lot—Roylin Bailey's Honda.

Hakeem cursed softly, and a vein in his temple jumped beneath his dark skin.

"Just ignore him," Darcy pleaded. "Everybody knows he's a loser."

The sun was going down, and it would be dark in about an hour. The pale outline of the full moon already hung ominously over the horizon. Everybody would be going home soon. *If only Roylin had just stayed away,* Darcy thought. *Everything was going so well.*

Roylin came to the edge of the picnic area and stood with his hands on his hips, his gaze roaming until it settled on Hakeem. "Oh, there's the retard," he called out. "H-H-Hakeem, h-h-how you doin', man? You learn to t-t-talk right yet? Huh? Huh?"

Hakeem scrambled to his feet.

"Hakeem! No!" Darcy cried.

With the speed of a big, lean cat, Hakeem lunged at Roylin. Roylin tried to block Hakeem's punches, but one connected with his nose, spraying droplets of blood on his white t-shirt. He seemed unprepared for Hakeem's rage. With a look of wild fear in his face, Roylin fled across the parking lot.

Darcy was not exactly sure what happened after that. A champagne-colored Nissan had come into the parking lot without anybody noticing it because all attention was on the fight. The Nissan screeched to a stop. Darcy heard Cooper scream, "They got guns!"

For a minute Darcy did not understand. Had Roylin pulled out a gun?

Then rapid shots crackled in the air like firecrackers. Everyone at the picnic ducked. As Darcy hit the grass to escape the gunfire, she saw guns flashing in the side windows of the Nissan.

Next to her, somebody was screaming, and the air was filled with the chaotic sounds of bursting cola bottles and splintering picnic tables. A bullet hit the trunk of a tree a few feet ahead of her, shattering the bark into small pieces. Darcy did not dare raise her head.

Mingled with the sounds of screaming and shouting was the wail of a police siren. Help was on the way. The Nissan's tires squealed as it raced from the parking lot.

The shots had stopped, and kids were getting up slowly like shadowy figures on a battlefield. The comforting aroma of the barbecue was quickly overwhelmed by the acrid stench of gun smoke. It was as if the party itself had been slain and now was broken and bleeding. Limp balloons lay like corpses on the grass, and one of Tarah's birthday gifts, a teddy bear, had been ripped into small pieces by the gunfire.

Darcy searched for Hakeem, finally finding him standing in the parking lot, blood on his shirt. "Hakeem! Are you okay?" she gasped.

Hakeem nodded. His eyes were strange, and his voice faltered. "Bailey got shot in the head. He was running from me."

Darcy followed his gaze and saw the crumpled figure in the parking lot, blood pouring from a head wound. It was Roylin. He was motionless, sprawled there, arms flung out, feet and legs hunched under him as if he crouched into a fetal position when he was hit.

"Oh my God," Hakeem said, "he was running from *me!*"

Everybody gathered around silently—Tarah, her cousins, the kids from the center, Cooper, Keisha, Shariff, Sonia, and all the others from school. Cooper threw an arm around Hakeem's shoulders. "Hey, man, wasn't your fault. He never shoulda been here. I seen Londell James in the Nissan. He's the one shot Bailey. Wasn't your fault."

The paramedics arrived within minutes and began working feverishly over Roylin Bailey, stabilizing him before carrying him into the ambulance.

"Nobody else got shot," Tarah said in a numb voice. "Just him. Why'd he have to be here? *Why?* Will somebody tell me that?"

Sonia's eyes were wide with disbelief. "Why did those guys shoot at us?"

"I let them know I wasn't invitin' no troublemakers, and this was Londell James's payback, that's what," Tarah said bitterly.

Darcy gave Tarah a long, silent hug, then returned to Hakeem's side. He turned and looked at Darcy. "*I got him shot.* If I'd kept my cool he never woulda got shot. Nobody else was hit, just him. He was an easy target, running in the parking lot by himself. It was *my* fault he was there. I got him shot." Hakeem shook his head slowly. His glazed eyes did not move or blink. It was as if he was watching something horrible happen in the distance, something he had no power to stop.

"Hakeem," Darcy whispered, "it wasn't your fault."

"His Mom. Bailey's Mom . . . she's single, and they got four younger kids. I don't know what she's gonna do. Roylin, he gave her money," Hakeem said, shaking his head and staring at the ground.

Darcy did not know what to say for a moment. Then she said, "Let's go to the hospital and see if there's anything we can do, Hakeem. Okay? Maybe we can help Mrs. Bailey."

Hakeem looked inspired by the suggestion. "Yeah. Yeah! C'mon, let's go right now."

When they got to the ER waiting room, Darcy and Hakeem found Mrs. Bailey and her children waiting for word on Roylin's condition. Amberlynn was clinging to her mother's shoulder and crying. Mrs. Bailey held a baby girl in her lap, and two little boys, about five or six, fought over a toy truck on the floor. Darcy sat down beside Mrs. Bailey. "I'm Darcy Wills and this is my friend, Hakeem Randall. We go to Bluford High with Roylin. We came down to see if there was anything we could do," Darcy said.

Mrs. Bailey looked stunned. Her two little boys were in a wild tug-of-war over the small truck, and the baby was crying. Hakeem leaned forward and said softly, "Mrs. Bailey, how about me taking the boys down to the cafeteria for some ice cream? There's a little play area down there where they can work off some steam."

"Thank you," Mrs. Bailey said, gladly turning the warring little boys over to Hakeem. He took each child by the hand, and they danced off with him, lured by the prospect of ice cream and play. Helping Mrs. Bailey seemed to calm Hakeem down too.

Darcy took the baby from Mrs. Bailey's arms and rocked her gently. "Have you heard anything about Roylin yet?" Darcy asked.

"No," Mrs. Bailey moaned, shaking her head. "I been sittin' here waiting ever since they called me. I was home with the children, and they called me. My sister drove me down right away, but then she hadda go back to work. They said the nurse would call me over to that window there when I could see my boy."

The baby settled down in Darcy's arms, and Mrs. Bailey dabbed at her red-rimmed eyes. "I couldn't believe my boy was shot. I just couldn' believe it. Roylin ain't no angel, but he never been mixed up with gangs. Why'd they shoot him? Why'd they go and shoot my boy for nothin'?"

Amberlynn had been sniffling softly, but now she looked at Darcy with big, soulful eyes. "Did my brother start the trouble at the party?" she asked.

"No," Darcy said. Roylin's teasing of Hakeem and their fight had nothing to do with the shooting. "Some thugs just drove by and started shooting, Amberlynn. It was just a stupid drive-by."

The nurse appeared at a small window. "Mrs. Bailey?" she called out.

Mrs. Bailey jumped up. "Oh Lord. Oh precious Lord—what if he's dead? What if my boy is *dead*?" Her eyes were wild with terror, and she was shaking violently.

Darcy put her free arm around the woman's shoulder and said, "It'll be okay, Mrs. Bailey. I'll pray real hard for you. You go on in, and I'll stay here with Amberlynn and the baby."

Mrs. Bailey hurried towards the door that opened into the emergency ward. Darcy sat down with the baby, and Amberlynn sat very close to them. After a few minutes, Amberlynn asked in a small voice, "Is Hakeem your boyfriend?"

"We're good friends," Darcy said as she rocked the baby in her arms.

"Roylin said he was retarded, but he's not, right?" Amberlynn asked.

"No, he's not. Sometimes, when he gets nervous, Hakeem stutters, but he's fine," Darcy said.

"I bet all this happened 'cause of Roylin being mean to somebody. He's awful mean, stomping on my stuffed animals and smashing my little brothers' toys. He yells at Mom and stuff too. He calls her bad names sometimes. Darcy, you think that's why he got shot, 'cause he's mean?" Amberlynn asked.

"No, it didn't happen because of Roylin being mean, Amberlynn. Some guys drove up and just shot at people at the party. I don't know why stuff like that happens. It's just awful," Darcy said.

Amberlynn played nervously with a shell bracelet on her wrist. "I know one thing. When I get old enough to have a real boyfriend, he won't be somebody like Roylin. Not me. I want a boy who's nice. Like Hakeem." Darcy smiled at her.

It seemed as if they waited forever in the crowded room. Darcy looked at the other people, an elderly man with a woman in a wheelchair, a gray-haired woman leading a man with a walker, young mothers with coughing babies, asthmatic kids wheezing. There were the relatives of accident victims, the parents of a teenager brought in comatose after a drug overdose. The parents looked so young themselves, and both were weeping.

Finally Hakeem returned to the waiting room with the boys. They were calmer, and they sat down quietly beside him. Hakeem turned anxiously to Darcy. "Did Mrs. Bailey go in?"

"Yeah, about fifteen minutes ago," Darcy answered. "I don't know if, you know, she can see him, or if they just want to talk to her . . . I mean . . ." Darcy didn't want to say the words. Was Roylin dead? Were the doctors telling Mrs. Bailey as kindly as they could that in spite of all their efforts, her son was dead and there were things she had to do, the stuff that has to be done when someone dies?

"I heard over the radio in the cafeteria that the police caught Londell James and the other guys in the car," Hakeem said. He shook his head. "All the shots went wild, all but the one that got Bailey. Why couldn't I just have ignored him? *Why?*"

"Hakeem, stop it. It wasn't your fault," Darcy said. "Roylin is a . . ." Darcy noticed Amberlynn staring at her and changed the subject. "I'm glad the police got the guys who shot at us. I hope they put them in jail forever!"

Suddenly Amberlynn said, "One time

last year Roylin ran away. He was gone a whole week. I was glad. Mama cried, but I was hoping he didn't come back 'cause it was so peaceful in our house. When Daddy lived with us, it was real bad, and then when Mama kicked Daddy out, Roylin took over messin' us up."

"I'm so sorry, Amberlynn," Darcy said, putting an arm around Amberlynn's shoulders.

"Know what?" Amberlynn continued. "Daddy used to whup Roylin up one side of his head and down the other. When Roylin didn't put out the garbage, Daddy whupped him for bein' lazy. When Roylin did put out the garbage, Daddy whupped him for doin' it wrong. Daddy was all the time yelling and beating his fists on the table and cussing out everybody. I guess that's what made Roylin so mean, but I don't care. I just kind of hate him 'cause I'm scared of him."

"No, Amberlynn, you don't hate him," Hakeem said. "Roylin's your blood, and that's thicker than anything."

Amberlynn's eyes widened again. "You think if he dies it'll be my fault 'cause I hate him?"

"No, no," Darcy said. "It's got nothing to do with you, Amberlynn."

Darcy thought about her own father. He was never like Roylin's dad. Carl Wills ran out on his family, true. But the years he was there were good ones. Suddenly she felt the need to hear her father's voice. "I need to make a phone call," Darcy said, gently placing the sleeping baby into Amberlynn's arms.

Darcy fumbled in her purse until she found the number her father had given her. She had used it just one time before: that bitter cold night when Jamee was lost in the mountains. Her father had come and found Jamee beside the giant cedar tree and probably saved her life. Now Darcy dialed the number again. It rang four times before he answered.

"Hi, this is Darcy," she said, her voice a little shaky. She could not believe she was so nervous talking to her own father.

"Is something wrong?" he asked quickly.

"No. I just wanted to tell you we could, you know, get together like you've been wanting. I mean if you still want to, just for hamburgers or something. I'd like to talk to you," Darcy said.

"Oh, that'd be great. Would Wednesday around six be okay for you?

If not, we could set another time, any time you want."

"Wednesday would be good," Darcy said. "At six."

"Oh, great. That's just great. So, see you then."

"Yeah," Darcy said.

"Bye, sweetheart," Darcy's father said.

Darcy took a deep breath. "Bye, Dad." She put the phone down quickly and returned to the waiting room.

Mrs. Bailey was coming from the emergency ward and heading for her children, tears running down her face.

Chapter 6

"Praise the Lord!" Mrs. Bailey cried. "He's gonna be all right! They're keepin' him here a few days, but they say the bullet just grazed his head and it did not hit his brain. Praise the Lord, my boy's gonna be all right!"

Darcy gave Mrs. Bailey a hug, and the woman said, "Thank you both for bein' here when I needed you so much. My sister is comin' over in a few minutes to get us all home. Bless you for all you did tonight. Roylin is mighty lucky to have friends like you at Bluford High. I never knew he had such good friends."

Darcy and Hakeem glanced at each other awkwardly. "Yeah, well, we're just glad Roylin will be okay," Hakeem said.

Gently, Darcy put her arm around Hakeem's shoulders and led him out the hospital exit and into the parking lot, where they walked to the silver motorbike. "Whew!" Hakeem said. "What a day! It would've haunted me for the rest of my life if Bailey hadn't made it. Man, I don't *ever* want something like that to happen again. My Dad always said only a fool settles stuff with violence, and I was too stupid to understand that until today."

They drove silently down the dark streets towards Darcy's. As they neared her home, Hakeem said, "You were great tonight. Thanks."

"Sure. 'Night," Darcy said. Then she kissed Hakeem on the cheek and ran up the walk to the door. Mom was doing the eleven-to-seven shift tonight, so she was home when Darcy went in.

"How was the birthday party, sweetie?" Mom asked.

Darcy sat on the couch near Mom's recliner. "Mom, everybody is okay, but something awful happened. There was a drive-by shooting, and the picnic got sprayed with bullets," Darcy said.

Mom clasped her hands to her cheeks and gasped, "Lord have mercy! Oh, sweetie, are you sure you're all right? Let me see you, baby! You okay?"

"I'm fine. Roylin Bailey got shot, but he's going to be okay. They got the guys who did it," Darcy said.

"Oh, baby," Mom sighed, tightly embracing Darcy. "If something happened to you or Jamee, I think I'd die. You hear me, sweetie? You be careful, hear?"

"Sure, Mom," Darcy said. She went to Grandma's room then. Grandma was sitting in a chair watching a quiz show on television.

Grandma laughed when somebody won something and bounced up and down in glee. She did not really understand what was going on, and she did not see much beyond people hopping around and screaming, but she seemed to enjoy the spectacle. When the show was over, Grandma talked about her childhood and how she dated Grandpa when they were both teenagers in the hills of Alabama. Darcy loved the stories. She knew every detail of them, but she still enjoyed hearing Grandma talk. About how young Annie, Grandma, was only fourteen in braids tied with pink ribbons when she held hands during Sunday services with her boyfriend, who was sixteen and six feet tall. About how Reverend Timsdale scolded them when he caught them and then winked and said he and Mrs. Timsdale were known to do the same thing when they were teenagers.

"I've sort of got a boyfriend, Grandma," Darcy confided. "His name is Hakeem, and he's really nice."

"Well, you're a wonderful girl, Angelcake," Grandma told her. Then her face clouded. "I wish it wasn't so dark in here so I could see you better."

Darcy almost pointed out that all the lights were on, but instead she said, "It's nighttime, Grandma. It'll be brighter in the morning."

"I hope so," Grandma said.

Darcy helped Grandma to bed and sat with her until she fell asleep. Then, with Grandma sleeping, Darcy whispered to her gently. "Don't you worry, Grandma, you'll never go to a nursing home. Never! It just won't happen. You'll stay right here with us. Nobody is ever gonna take you away from us, except God. He's the only one gonna take you away from us, Grandma!"

On Monday, everybody at Bluford High was talking about the shooting. Londell James was over eighteen, so he was being charged as an adult with attempted murder. "I hope those punks get locked up for so long that they'll be eligible for parole when they're on social security!" Tarah said.

Darcy and Tarah had joined a group of students gathered outside the library talking about the shooting. In the crowd, Darcy recognized Brisana's voice. "Oh, Hakeem, to think you might have been killed in that awful shooting! I could just die to even think of it! I'm so glad you're okay!"

"Yeah," Hakeem said. "Roylin Bailey is gonna be okay too. A bullet grazed his head, but he'll be fine."

"Like anybody cares," Brisana replied. Then she added, "Oh, by the way, Hakeem, I was telling my Dad what a great singer and guitar player you are, and he wondered if you'd like to use my older brother's guitar for the audition. It's practically brand new, and I think it would make your songs even better."

"But what about your brother?" Hakeem asked. "Does he want some guy he doesn't even know messing with his guitar?"

Brisana laughed. "Michael has lost interest in music. His guitar is just sitting there gathering dust. Hakeem, with your talent and this guitar, you're going to just blow everybody else away at the auditions!"

"Well . . . thanks, Brisana," Hakeem said awkwardly.

"Maybe you could come over one day after school to pick it up," Brisana suggested, twirling her hair with her finger.

"Sure, I definitely will."

"Maybe I could cook something for you to eat while you're there. I'm a great cook."

"Umm . . ." Hakeem hesitated. "Well, okay. That sounds cool."

Darcy watched Hakeem and Brisana from a distance. They did not see her in the crowd of students, but she could see them. Brisana was wearing a pink cropped top and really tight jeans. She had a great figure, and Hakeem was checking her out. *He is a normal guy, isn't he,* Darcy reasoned. *Of course he would look at a girl like Brisana, but did his eyes have to crawl all over her like that?*

Darcy waited until Brisana walked away, and then she joined Hakeem.

"Hey," said Hakeem, "I heard that Roylin got out of the hospital already.

His head is all bandaged, but he's doing okay."

"Yeah," Darcy said, "they don't keep people in the hospital any longer than they have to. Mom tells me that guys are out of the hospital in a few days even after serious heart operations."

"I'm sure glad Roylin made out okay. Man, that was close," Hakeem said, shaking his head. "Hey, you free to go out after school today? I thought we'd grab some tacos and go down to the beach and maybe watch the sun go down or something."

Darcy groaned. "Oh, that sounds so great, but I can't. Mom is working the early shift—four to midnight—and she's got to leave early to do paperwork. I've got to be there for Grandma. The lady who's been helping us out has a bad cold, so she can't come over. I don't want to leave Jamee alone with Grandma."

"Well, we'll do it another time," Hakeem said, but he looked disappointed. "There'll be plenty of afternoons."

Darcy was miserable as she sat down in English class. She *so* wanted to go to the beach with Hakeem and watch the sunset. It was the first time he had ever suggested doing something that romantic together. If only Ms. Harris did not have that cold so she could sit with Grandma.

And then it came over Darcy. Like a draft seeping through a crack in the wall you never even knew was there, Aunt Charlotte's words came back to her. "*It's just so hard and unfair that Darcy must be a baby-sitter and nurse every day for an old woman.*"

Darcy barely heard any of Mr. Keenan's lecture. She wondered if Tarah might possibly be free this afternoon to stay with Grandma. They would pay Tarah, of course, like they paid Ms. Harris. Hope surged in Darcy's heart. Maybe there was still a chance to watch the sun go down at Hakeem's side.

As class ended, Darcy hurried to talk to Tarah. In a frantic rush of words, she explained her predicament. "Oh, Tarah, if only you could—"

"Girl, I'm really sorry," Tarah cut in. "You know I'd do anything for you, but I got me that job down at the donut shop, and if I'm not there right after school, they'll can me in a second."

"Oh," Darcy said. "I didn't know you were working."

"My Daddy says to me I better start makin' some money 'cause he ain't payin' for no more clothes for me, and if I don't buy my own, I'll hafta go to school in my sister's old clothes. You hear what I'm sayin'? I could end up coming to school in stuff my sister tossed five years ago!" Tarah exclaimed.

All the rest of the day Darcy grieved for her lost opportunity to have that wonderful date with Hakeem. She hurried home from school brimming with a resentment she never felt before.

Mom was already at the door in her uniform, twirling her car keys, anxious to leave. "I gotta go, honey. Paperwork is piling up like a mound of snow after a blizzard. That place is a madhouse. The new administrator is watching us all like a hawk. She's just hoping somebody makes a mistake so she can write them up and get them fired. It'd help their bottom line if they could fire some experienced nurses and put younger, cheaper nursing assistants in their places."

After Mom left, Darcy tried to put Hakeem out of her mind. She decided to put the final touches on her astronomy project. She had built a small cardboard model of a human settlement on Mars.

She was carefully painting the model's tiny buildings when she heard Grandma yell from her bedroom, "I'm tired of laying around!"

Darcy went into Grandma's room to find her trying to get out of bed by herself. Grandma was in one of her cranky moods. "I can take care of my own self," she muttered. "I don't need no help. What do you think I am? I been taking care of myself for a lotta years, and I don't need no help now." She almost fell to the floor as she waved Darcy off.

"Grandma, no!" Darcy said sharply. "Let me bring the walker!"

"The walker?" Grandma grumbled. "I never heard of such a thing! Since when do I need a walker? You trying to make an invalid out of me? When did I ever need a walker? I think it's time I got my own place. Don't need all this fussing over me!"

"Grandma, please!" Darcy cried as the woman tried to get up, driving Darcy away with flailing arms. Darcy grabbed the walker and brought it close, banging it against the frame of the bed. She was surprised at how angry she was feeling. "Do what I tell you, Grandma, or you're gonna hurt yourself! You'll fall down!"

Grandma's arms continued to flail around, and she slapped Darcy's cheek. Darcy rubbed her cheek, and tears of frustration gathered in her eyes.

Suddenly Darcy hated everything about the darkened room—the heavy scent of lilac powder, the metal cans of nutrition drink, the overpowering sense of loss. And she hated having to struggle with Grandma, an old woman striking out against a world she could no longer handle.

Darcy wanted to be on the beach, kicking off her shoes and running over the cool sand, her arm linked with Hakeem's. She wanted to be sitting beside him while the wind, salt-scented and sharp, whipped her hair and the sunset bathed them in golden light.

Darcy felt trapped. It would always be this way, she thought, and sooner or later Hakeem would sense it too. She was sure that he would grow tired of waiting for her and that he would become interested in someone else, someone who was free, attractive, and smart. Someone like Brisana.

Chapter 7

After Darcy got Grandma to the bathroom and back, the old woman fell asleep. Darcy knew there would be no apology from Grandma later. Her grandmother probably would not even remember the ugly incident.

Darcy returned to the kitchen where Jamee sat reading a magazine about her favorite rap stars, her head wrapped in a giant bath towel.

"Where have *you* been?" Darcy snapped. "You know you *could* help with Grandma once in a while."

"I was in the shower!" Jamee yelled. "And I did spend time with Grandma today. I got home early from school, and I took her for a ride in her wheelchair. We went all the way down to the park. She listened to the birds singing and had a really good time," Jamee said defensivel

"Well maybe that's why she was in such a bad mood. She isn't used to so much excitement, and she got confused and angry," Darcy grumbled.

"Man," Jamee fumed, "I can't do *anything* right, can I? Why don't you just go to France with old Aunt Charlotte? You're getting just like her. We'll get along fine without you."

Darcy slumped into a kitchen chair. "I had a real bad day," she confessed. In the old days Jamee would not accept an apology. Now she was more mellow.

"Yeah, I get those days too," Jamee said, sounding for the moment even older than her fourteen years. "Days that make you want to scream as loud as you can, no matter who's watching. Like when I do bad on some stupid test or get zits right when I'm trying to look good for Tyrone."

Darcy smiled a little. "You know what? I'm finally going to dinner with Dad," she said.

"Get out of here," Jamee cried. "Are you serious? That's great! When are you going?"

"Wednesday. At six. I'm really nervous," Darcy said. "I guess I don't know how to act around him since he came back. He's our dad, but it doesn't feel right."

"Darcy, know what? I heard him and Mom talking on the phone about going to one of those marriage counselors. Dad wants to, but Mom doesn't. I don't know if it'd be good or not. I just wish . . ." Jamee struggled for words. "I just don't want Mom to grow old alone. She needs someone. If it's not Dad, then it'd be somebody else, and I wouldn't like that, would you?"

"No," Darcy admitted. "I guess I wouldn't."

"You know," Jamee said, "I'm so glad you're going to dinner with Dad. When we went to dinner the other day, Dad kept going on and on about how he was scared you'd never forgive him. He was just hoping so much that you'd talk to him."

Darcy knew Jamee secretly hoped that somehow the family would come together again. *Of course it can never be like before,* Darcy thought. But how different would it be? Like Grandma said, "*Life is full of hurts, Angelcake. But they always make us stronger if we learn from them.*"

It was hard for Darcy to get to sleep that night. She kept imagining how the beach date with Hakeem might have gone. And then she had a fitful dream about it. She and Hakeem were walking hand in hand across the cooling beach, and the sun was going down quickly, turning the water crimson. They were walking together toward the water, into the blazing red sunset. Hakeem stopped and rolled up the legs of his jeans and they went into the water and the foamy sea lapped at their ankles. Darcy shouted to Hakeem to be careful, but he let go of her hand and kept walking into the surf. He went out farther and farther until the glowing sky and the sparkling waves seemed to swallow him up. Darcy screamed Hakeem's name as he started to swim towards the horizon. She stared after him, the dying sun blinding her, until she could not see him anymore. She was overcome with a numbing desolation—he was gone. Hakeem was gone.

Then Darcy awoke with a start. She could hear Grandma mumbling about Alabama in the next room. Grandma seemed to be all right, so Darcy did not get up. Grandma often mumbled in her sleep.

Darcy tried to get back to sleep, but she kept thinking about Hakeem. How much longer would he remain interested in her if she never had time for him?

The next morning, Darcy tried to eat the scrambled eggs and bacon that Mom made, but she could hardly get them down. She was not superstitious, but the dream troubled her. Losing Hakeem to the sea seemed like some terrible omen. Darcy was eager to get to school and be reassured that everything was all right between them.

Darcy was almost at Bluford when another girl walked alongside her. She was in two classes with Darcy, but they were not friends. The girl's eyes gleamed with excitement over the gossip she was eager to share. "I thought you and Hakeem Randall were sort of going together," she began.

"We're friends," Darcy said quickly, trying to head off the gossip.

"Yeah, well, Tarah Carson said you guys were going together, and so I was really surprised when Brisana told me she and Hakeem went to the beach yesterday afternoon." The girl stared expectantly at Darcy, obviously waiting for her reaction.

Darcy gave her a steely look and shrugged. "I guess it's still a free country. Hakeem can do anything he wants."

Darcy walked on alone then, her insides churning with hurt. Was Hakeem so shallow that he turned right around and asked Brisana to that romantic beach date?

At lunchtime, Hakeem and Cooper came walking up to where Darcy and Tarah were eating. The boys were talking about music. Cooper was singing the praises of rap, and Hakeem was saying that soft, smooth ballads had more lasting impact. "My Grandpa said that Nat King Cole was the best singer he ever heard," Hakeem said.

"I do give him credit for his time, man," Cooper conceded, "but he's not for now. Music today tells what's goin' on in the 'hood. I can relate to it more than some old guy singin' about stuff that went down fifty years ago."

"C'mon, man," Hakeem smiled. "You need to open your mind to something different."

"Yeah, maybe when I'm an old dude myself," Cooper laughed.

"So," Darcy said matter-of-factly, "did you get to do anything yesterday afternoon, Hakeem?"

"Oh, yeah. It worked out real good," Hakeem answered.

"I was sorry I had to go home early," Darcy said, "but Grandma needed me." She struggled to keep the bitterness out of her voice. "I'm glad you didn't waste the afternoon."

Before Hakeem could say anything else, two guys from the track team came over to the table and announced that the team was having a meeting during lunch.

"I guess I gotta go," Hakeem said reluctantly, getting up from the table.

"Coop and I gotta go too, Tarah said, smiling at Cooper. "Coop's got a test in his next class, and we're gonna make sure he gets a B. I'll catch up with you after lunch," she explained.

Cooper pushed his chair away from the table and stood up. "Girl, you are worse than my momma," he said as he walked off.

For an instant, Darcy was completely alone at the table, and then she spotted Brisana walking toward her, a tight-lipped smile on her face. Darcy rolled her eyes and braced herself.

"I guess you heard about me and Hakeem," Brisana said.

"Excuse me?" Darcy said, flipping through her science textbook. "Can we talk about this later? I've got some reading to do."

"Hakeem and I went to the beach and went swimming," Brisana purred, "and, oh, it was so romantic."

"I can't imagine why you're telling me all this," Darcy replied coolly.

Brisana came closer. "Don't give me that, Darcy. You're *crazy* about Hakeem, but he doesn't feel that way about you. You're just another girl to him, and not a very special one either. So now you know how it feels to be dumped. You and I, we were friends, and you dropped me the second you got your trashy new friends."

Darcy looked up, surprised by the rage on Brisana's face. "I didn't dump you. I wanted us to stay friends. You stopped being *my* friend when I started talking to Tarah and Cooper and those other kids. I mean, you wanted it to be just us, but I didn't want to shut out everybody else."

"You *knew* how I felt about those two losers—you *knew* it'd ruin our friendship if you dragged them in. It was like inviting ants to a picnic!" Brisana's voice trembled with anger. "You knew, but you did it anyway. You were my only close friend. You dumped me so you could get in solid with a bunch of trash. Well, now you know what it feels like to have a special friend you trust and then have that friend ditch you!" Brisana turned quickly and stalked off.

Darcy was amazed. She had always thought of Brisana as a tough, arrogant person whose feelings never seemed to get hurt. But now that she thought about it, Darcy realized that she never really knew Brisana. They were each other's lunch companion since freshman year at Bluford. But in all that time, Darcy thought, they had never talked about deep things, real things. They had just been someone for the other person to be with to keep from eating alone.

But am I to blame? Darcy asked herself, *Brisana brought it on herself!* She could have joined Darcy and her new friends. It was *her* choice, *her* decision.

When Darcy found Tarah, she told her everything that had happened. "Girl," Tarah said, "she's hurtin'. Even mean people hurt. Maybe they hurt worse than anybody. So what you gotta do is reach out to her."

"Tarah!" Darcy almost shrieked. "She's bragging about going to the beach with Hakeem! I just about hate her! She said she and Hakeem were swimming—"

"Oh, come on, girl, it's fifty-something degrees in the water," Tarah laughed. "You know about that girl and her wild imagination."

"But I know she was out with him, and I'm sure they walked the beach together, and—"

"Darcy Wills, you set yourself down and listen up," Tarah commanded. "Hakeem told Coop that Brisana told him he could pick up her brother's guitar yesterday since he wasn't doing anything else. Now, what don't you understand about *that*?"

"You mean . . . she was lying about the beach?"

"Hello? Lights comin' on in your brain, girl? She is so lonesome and angry all she knows how to do now is hurt other people. You think you are big enough to look past all she's done and try to make her better, Darcy? I'm gonna be real disappointed if you say no 'cause that means you ain't as special as I always figured," Tarah said.

Darcy shrugged.

"C'mon, let's go to class," Tarah said, putting her arm around Darcy's shoulder and leading her forward.

After school, Darcy heard guitar music coming from the courtyard behind the library. She walked over and found Hakeem sitting on a bench practicing on the new guitar. Nearby, Brisana pretended she was reading a book, but from time to time she glanced at Hakeem and Darcy.

"Hi, Hakeem," Darcy said. "You sound great."

"It's this guitar. Makes a big difference," he explained.

"Brisana's brother's guitar, huh?"

"Yeah, we got it yesterday."

Darcy looked over at Brisana and shouted, "Hey, Brisana!"

Brisana hesitated. Darcy could imagine what was going through her mind. *What is Darcy up to now? She's found out from Hakeem that we didn't have that romantic beach date, and now she wants to humiliate me.* Brisana got up slowly, walking warily towards Hakeem and Darcy. She looked nervous, defensive.

"This guitar is so great, Brisana," Darcy said warmly. "I mean, it was really nice that you let Hakeem have it. Doesn't he sound good when he plays? Much better than on his other guitar."

Brisana stared at Darcy, then at Hakeem. "Uh, I'm glad it's working out," she mumbled.

"Yeah, it's real smooth. Thanks a lot, Brisana," Hakeem said.

"Brisana, I'm practicing for the auditions too, only I don't know what to sing. The auditorium is probably empty right now, and I was thinking of going over there and trying out a couple of songs. Would you come listen and tell me which song sounds better?" Darcy asked.

"*Me*?"

"Yeah, if you've got the time. I mean, I'm embarrassed to try out my songs in front of anybody else, but you've known me long enough to see me being stupid plenty of times," Darcy said.

A tiny smile flickered in Brisana's eyes. "Okay. Let's go. But if you stink, you know I'll tell you."

Darcy and Brisana walked towards the auditorium with Darcy chattering the whole time. "I wanted to sing something new. But Hakeem says I should do a classic song, and my Mom wants me to sing this old Aretha Franklin song from when she was a kid. There's no way I can sing like her!"

Darcy nervously mounted the stage with an audience of one—Brisana. Darcy tried her best to get her voice to sound like Aretha Franklin's. As she finished, Brisana howled, "Give me a break! Oh, that's so awful that if you sing it, you'll never live it down! You'll have to wear a brown paper bag over your head for the rest of the year."

"That bad, huh?" Darcy groaned.

"Let's hear one of those songs you did at the freshman talent show ages ago. You did a Supremes song—'Stop! In the Name of Love.' Try that."

Darcy's self-confidence was shattered, but she did remember doing a pretty good job on that old Supremes song. She sang it for Brisana as best she could.

Brisana didn't say anything during the song, but when Darcy finished, she said, "That might work. You'll have to practice a lot more, but it's not horrible."

Darcy was very relieved. Now, at least, she knew what she would sing at the auditions. She did not expect to get into the talent show, but at least she would not make a fool of herself.

"Thanks a lot, Brisana. Hey, I got some time before I have to go home. Want to get a sundae?"

"Our regular sinful sundae with butterscotch and nuts on top?"

"Yeah!"

They hurried down the street and settled into the booth on the side where they always used to sit. "Oh, man," Darcy said, "I haven't had one of these since . . . you know."

"I know," Brisana said. She looked right at Darcy, "I just don't like your new friends. I just don't."

"I've missed you, Brisana. Maybe—"

"We used to be *such* good friends, Darcy," Brisana interrupted, spinning her spoon around in the sundae. "Then all of a sudden you just dropped me, like I never existed."

"That's not true," Darcy began calmly. "We never knew Tarah and Cooper, but we said bad things about them anyway. Well, I got to know them and found out that they were really nice. I gave them a chance. You never tried to."

Brisana shifted her eyes to her melting mush of ice cream.

"Maybe we could get some time together like in the old days, just us,"

Darcy said.

"Yeah, that'd be okay. I'd like that," Brisana replied.

"And we could go to the mall again."

Brisana smiled. "Yeah. Man, this sundae is *sooo* good. I haven't enjoyed anything like this in a long time."

Darcy smiled back at Brisana. Brisana did not mean she was enjoying only the sundae, but she would never admit it. And Darcy would let it go at that. Like Tarah said once while they were helping set up a neighborhood garden on her block, "Friendships are like trees. If you give them time and space to grow, they'll get stronger and stronger."

Darcy jogged past the familiar landmarks on the way home—the Asian market, the restaurants. They were all blurs as she ran. She did not want Mom to be late for work, and she had dawdled over that butterscotch sundae too long.

"I'm home, Mom," Darcy yelled as she came in the front door.

"Okay, baby." Mom did not seem as rushed as usual. In fact, she looked relaxed. Her hair was freshly done, and she was wearing a flattering new shade of lipstick.

"Mom, you look great!" Darcy exclaimed.

Mom giggled. She looked younger than she had in years. "Oh, get out of here, girl. I'm the same old same old."

Darcy watched her mother go out to the car. Was it possible she was meeting someone during her break tonight? She always ate a snack in the cafeteria, and once or twice Dad met her there. Would she be trying to look extra nice for him? After all that had happened, would she be doing that? Or was there someone else? Had seeing Dad again and facing the past helped her to realize that it would never work the second time around?

Maybe that handsome Jamaican RN who called her mother a few months ago was back in the picture. Or perhaps that retired doctor had returned to the hospital to visit one of his former patients.

Darcy felt nervous. She did not know if it was better to conjure up a new man for her mother or hope for her father's return to the household. Still, if it became absolutely certain that they could never be a family again, something inside Darcy would die.

Chapter 8

In Bluford High's auditorium at lunchtime, about fifty students auditioned for the talent show. Teachers from the drama and music departments were judging the performances. Darcy had practiced her song many times, but when her turn came, she felt as if she were going to her execution. She almost stumbled going up the three steps to the stage. She did not care at this point if she earned a place in the talent show. She just did not want to embarrass herself too much. And she wanted to get it over with.

Darcy sang "Stop! In the Name of Love," and when she finished the last line, she was shocked to hear applause.

"All right!" Hakeem said when she reached her seat. Darcy was overwhelmed with relief that she could now sit and watch everybody else.

A sophomore performed spoken poetry filled with rhymes straight off a rap CD. A number of students clapped when she finished. A freshman boy performed an embarrassingly bad comic skit involving a puppet, and there was hardly any applause at all. Then, finally, it was time for Hakeem to go on stage. He strode towards the stage with authority, his guitar on his back. He stood silent a moment, his head down; then he brought the guitar around, strumming out a pounding rhythm to a song Darcy had never heard him sing before.

> *Gotta live until I die, don't nobody*
> *take me out before my time.*
> *Gunshots in the night,*
> *You know this can't be right!*
> *Listen up, take my hand, help me*
> *when I make my stand.*
> *Gotta rise, gotta sing, sing so strong,*
> *Drown the sorrow with my song,*
> *Take back the day, take back the*
> *night,*
> *With our hearts and our voices,*
> *we'll win this fight!*

The applause began during the song, and kids were clapping their hands and stomping their feet to the driving cry of anger and pain. Darcy knew what Hakeem was trying to say in his song, but she wondered if the other students understood him. Not everyone had seen Roylin get shot. And many kids were too young to know Russell Walker, the boy gunned down last year. Still, as she watched, Darcy could see that Hakeem was stirring the crowd with his guitar and his voice.

Slowly, one by one, students stood up, pressing their palms skyward in a gesture of enthusiastic approval. Their faces told Darcy they were not just supporting the young man on the stage. They were also cheering for his tribute to all the shattered lives on the street, all the little kids afraid to go out and play, all their friends and relatives who had suffered, all the young people who had paid the ultimate price.

Darcy felt tears streaming down her face. She was so happy for Hakeem. She had been hoping and praying he would do well, but she had never expected such a performance and such a reaction.

Outside the auditorium in the afternoon, the names of the students who would be in the talent show were posted.

Darcy did not make it, but she was not disappointed. She enjoyed singing, but she did not like public solos. Hakeem would, of course, be in the talent show. Students crowded around him, congratulating him.

"You were wonderful," Darcy said, managing to get through his other admirers. Hakeem smiled and winked. But all the attention appeared to make him a little nervous. He was stuttering a bit. He escaped to the track to get in some laps.

Darcy's dinner with her father was that evening, and as the time drew near, her anxiety increased. She sat in the front window of the apartment waiting for the silver Toyota to pull up. He came at ten minutes to six, and Darcy jumped up. "I'm going now, Mom," she said. Her mother had the night off.

"Have a nice time, sweetie," Mom replied.

As Darcy sat down in her father's car, she noticed right away that Dad looked more fit than when he first arrived in town. He was trimmer and also more neatly dressed.

"Hi," Darcy said, buckling her seat belt. "You look like you lost some weight."

A nervous smile raced across his face. "Yeah. I've been working out at the gym, trying to lose my spare tire and get back some muscle tone. Been layin' off the cheeseburgers too."

"That's good," Darcy said. "It's healthier." She felt so stiff, so awkward. She could not have felt worse if she were going to dinner with Mr. Keenan, her English teacher.

"You're looking good, Darcy. A little too skinny maybe. Do you like Chinese food?"

"I think so," Darcy said. "I haven't had much of it."

"I know a nice little Chinese restaurant. Healthy and delicious," Dad assured her. He seemed as nervous as she was. It was hard to believe this was the warm, funny father Darcy used to love being with when she was eleven years old. It was as if those five years he was away had dug a huge chasm between them, and neither of them knew how to jump across.

"How is school going, Darcy?" he asked.

"Okay. I'm doing okay in everything. I just finished my astronomy project, and the teacher liked it."

"I suppose you have lots of nice friends," he said.

"A few." Five years ago, Darcy would have told him about Hakeem, but talking to him now about something personal seemed as awkward as sharing make-up secrets with a stranger. Darcy felt deeply sad. She wondered if it would be this way from now on, if something had happened in those five years that could never be repaired.

They pulled into the restaurant parking lot and went into a small, lovely place with dramatic paintings of red dragons on the walls. The chairs were red leather, and wonderful fragrances floated from the kitchen.

After they were seated, Darcy looked at the menu. "I guess when I think of Chinese food, I think of chop suey or something."

Dad smiled. It was his first real smile since the evening had started. Darcy realized all this was even more difficult for him than it was for her. He was the bad guy. He carried the guilt for what had happened. "This one, number four, that's excellent," he said.

Darcy read the English section of the menu: "Garlic sautéed scallops and shrimp, seasonal greens, eggplant, Szechuan. It sounds good," she said, "I just hope it doesn't taste like something

Aunt Charlotte would serve up." Darcy heard an odd noise, and she looked up to see her father laughing. She laughed a little too. Apparently, Dad remembered those once-a-month treks to Aunt Charlotte's and how the family would spend the whole trip home dissing the awful food.

"Oh my," Dad said, shaking his head sympathetically, "you still go over there, do you? And she's still making those concoctions?"

"Yeah." Darcy chuckled. "She takes all these gourmet cooking classes—she's smart and everything, but it never comes out right."

"Do you remember the octopus?" Dad asked.

"Yeah," Darcy said, starting to laugh again. "I couldn't get my fork into that rubbery thing, and Jamee, she was about five, I think, and she goes 'What's this stuff?' and Aunt Charlotte says 'It's a delicacy—it's octopus,' and Jamee starts throwing up under the table!"

"And the cucumber soup," Dad gasped, wiping his eyes after tears of laughter.

"And the fish that smelled so bad that the people in the next townhouse complained," Darcy giggled.

For just a few minutes it was like old times, but then Darcy remembered the distance between them. To break the awkward silence that suddenly set in, Darcy asked, "How's your job?"

"Good. I sell men's clothing, you know. The store is nice. My schedule is perfect, and I'm making good money."

"That's great. I always thought you were a good salesman."

Dad smiled and then clenched his hands in his lap. Whenever he had something difficult to say, he did that. Darcy did the same thing. "Darcy, how is your Grandma doing?"

"Pretty good. She's almost normal sometimes, for a little while, but mostly she's frail and kinda confused. But we all help take care of her, and it works out all right," Darcy answered. She felt tense. What was her father driving at? Was he, like Aunt Charlotte, going to suggest putting Grandma in a nursing home?

"The thing is, I was wondering what I could do to help," Dad stated. "There must be something."

"Mom said you're already helping out with money," Darcy said.

"I mean, I'd be willing to pay for every-thing, and your Mom could quit her job and—"

"Mom told me she'd never quit her job," Darcy interrupted.

"Yes, she told me that too. I thought you might try to convince her," Dad said, looking intently at Darcy.

Darcy looked down at the tablecloth, not knowing what to say. The truth was that Mom did not trust him. Darcy did not really trust him either. *Could Dad possibly be giving Mom enough money to quit her job?* Darcy wondered. Not wanting to ask him directly, she said, "I guess it'll take time, you know, for Mom to be able to do something like quit her job."

"I understand that, believe me, I do. And I don't blame her. But I love your Mom. I know that sounds phony after what happened, but it's true. And I love both you girls too . . . very much."

A cruel response threatened to fly from Darcy's lips. *Oh, really, Dad? Is that why you ran away with a twenty-four-year-old woman? Is that why you abandoned us?* But she said nothing.

"I know I haven't acted in a loving way," he went on. "I can't take away the hurt I caused. It happened. There are no excuses. There were problems in our marriage, but I took the coward's way out. Sometimes when things are not going great and a temptation comes to a person, it is so powerful. *So powerful.* You decide in a moment of—I don't know—craziness or something, you decide that this one thing is what's going to put everything right. You forget all the decent things you've always believed in, and you tell yourself you deserve this happiness. Suddenly you are feeling young and alive like you haven't felt in years, and . . ." The words came out slowly, painfully, like nails being pulled from a hard, dry board. "And then when the fire dies out, you are left with the ashes. Then you ache with guilt, and you realize you've hurt the people dearest to you, and you can't take it back." Darcy noticed that her father's eyes were bright with unshed tears.

"Why didn't you come back sooner, Dad? You just up and disappear for five years and expect everything to be all right?" Darcy asked.

"No, no, that's not it. Darcy, I just didn't have the courage to face what I'd done to my family, and I started drinking. I crawled into the bottle because I was a coward. I was in and out of a dozen detox centers. Every time I decided to come home, I'd lose the courage again. I'd think to myself, 'What does that family need with a worthless drunk? Haven't I hurt them enough?' Then I'd drink myself blind again. And then one day—I guess it was a stroke of fate, or maybe a blow from the Good Lord—I got stabbed in an alley, and I almost bled to death." He pointed to a scar near his left eye. "Almost got blinded. I decided to get sober and stay sober, and somehow I did. And then, when I was sure it was for real, I came home."

"Well, Dad, I don't know how all this is gonna play out. I'm not even sure how I want it to go. But for what it's worth, I'm glad you decided to come back," Darcy said.

He reached over and grasped her hand, giving it a squeeze. It was the first time her father had touched her since the goodbye hug those many years ago.

After dinner, Darcy and her father had another cup of coffee. "Maybe your Mom and I will go for counseling," he said. "I know things can't go back to the way they were, but I'll do anything it takes to become part of this family again. I'd like to take care of my family the way I used to. I'd like a chance to make up, to try to make up." His voice shook as he spoke. He was a big man, and there was something terrible about hearing his voice shake. It was like seeing a mighty oak tree waver in the wind, making you wonder if almost anything in the world might crash at some point.

Chapter 9

On Thursday, Roylin Bailey came back to school. His head was still bandaged from the injury. He seemed sobered by the experience. After English class, he hesitated before approaching Hakeem and Darcy in the hallway.

"How's it goin'?" he asked.

"Okay," Darcy said. "Glad to see you back in school. You feeling okay?"

"Yeah. Headache is about gone." Roylin glanced at Darcy and Hakeem. "Mom says you guys were a big help that first night."

"Well, your Mom had her hands full with the little kids," Darcy replied.

"Yeah, well," Roylin said. He looked as if he wanted to apologize for some of the things he said to Hakeem before, but he could not quite bring it off. Not yet. Maybe later on, but not yet. So Roylin just smiled a little, shrugged, and walked away. Darcy glanced at Hakeem. He looked distracted. Maybe he was thinking about the fight again, how close he came to carrying a burden of guilt, deserved or not, for the rest of his life.

Hakeem had not said anything about going out in quite some time. She wondered if it was all the pressure of preparing for the talent show, or maybe his father's illness. "Everything okay with you, Hakeem?" Darcy asked as they walked towards their next class.

"Yeah. Dad's going in for a checkup. Hope that turns out okay," Hakeem said.

A couple of girls from the cheerleading squad came running up to Hakeem. They told him he was sure to win the talent show. Hakeem smiled at them, his gaze seeming to linger on them as they skipped away. Or maybe that was just Darcy's imagination. If Hakeem won the talent show, pretty girls from Bluford would be all over him. He was only human. Darcy figured she might not look all that appealing to him anymore.

Darcy had wanted a boyfriend for such a long time, and her shyness had stood in the way. She really cared about Hakeem, but if he did not like her back, well, then, she would have to get past it. Like Grandma used to say before her stroke, *"Life for most of us is lots of potholes and ruts, and we got to get past them and keep moving on. That's the thing, keep moving on, our heads held high."*

Darcy tried to hold onto Grandma's words for comfort. But the thought of Hakeem losing interest in her cast a shadow on her heart. And there would not be any words comforting enough to lift it.

When Darcy got home from school that day, Mom was finishing a cup of coffee before leaving for the hospital. "Sweetie, I didn't get a chance to ask you—how was dinner with your father?"

"Good, Mom. I had a nice talk with him. He'd like to, you know, be more involved with the family again."

Mom set her coffee cup down hard. "Anything's possible, I guess. But don't expect too much, hear?" Mom paused. "It's not that I'm still angry—well, not much anyway. But that's not the main thing. What if I trusted him again and he went away again? Baby, I got a life now— *we've* got a life. It's not a great life, but at least I got some control. I know your father's real sorry for what he did, but I just can't put our lives back in that man's hands. Not yet. Maybe not ever."

"I understand, Mom," Darcy assured her.

"Sweetie, don't get me wrong. He is your father, and he'll always be your father. I'm not standing in the way of any relationship he wants to build with you girls. As a matter of fact, that's the one good thing I do hope comes out of all this. But as far as him stepping right back into being my husband—well, that's a whole 'nother story. We'll just take that one real slow for now, okay?"

About twenty minutes after Mom left, Jamee came home from school. She flung her backpack on the kitchen table, poured herself a glass of orange juice, and sat down. "Tyrone picked me to be his project partner in history class. We're gonna do a report on the guillotine. That's the big blade they used to chop people's heads off during the French Revolution. He is so hyped about it. Why are boys so *weird*?"

Darcy shrugged. "How should I know? Look at Hakeem. He acts like I don't even exist sometimes."

"Figures!" Jamee responded. "Boys only want to be bothered with you when they want you. Then you're supposed to drop everything you're doing and go running to see them. Tyrone's famous for that. We can be having a deep conversation, and if one of his boys comes along, he'll drop me right in the middle of a sentence to start talking about cars and stereo systems."

"I would say it'll get better as they get older, but looking at Mom, I'm not counting on it," Darcy observed.

"Do you think Mom and Dad are any closer to getting back together? He said he wants to get us a house. Girl, can't you just see the parties we could throw in a big backyard? It'd be good for Grandma too. She could sit out on the patio in her wheelchair and listen to the birds. Remember how she used to like to do that in her own yard?"

Darcy glanced out the window. There was plenty of daylight left to take Grandma down to the park for a little while if she was up to it.

Darcy helped Grandma into a sweater and then into the wheelchair. They went down in the elevator and out onto the street. "Are you warm enough,

Grandma?" Darcy asked, adjusting her sweater.

"Oh, it's so nice out," Grandma said contentedly.

Darcy pushed the elderly woman down the sidewalk to the tiny park at the corner. It was not much more than a few stone benches and some large mulberry trees, but you could always count on hearing the birds singing and chattering as they scrambled through the branches.

"Do you hear the birds, Grandma?" Darcy asked as she sat down on a bench by Grandma's wheelchair.

"I hear them. I put out the seed for them yesterday. There were starlings and some little sparrows. Oh, Angelcake, did you check the feeders this morning? I hope them greedy pigeons didn't get it all . . ." Grandma fretted. "And the birdbath. I cleaned it yesterday, but it gets dirty so quickly. And the starlings just have to take their morning bath. It just wouldn't do for the water to be dirty when they came." Grandma thought she was back at her little house again, sitting in her garden where bird feeders hung from every tree and a large stone birdbath dominated the middle of the yard.

"I took care of everything, Grandma," Darcy said. Just then Keisha, a girl from Darcy's science class, appeared with her grandfather walking slowly beside her, his hand in the crook of her arm.

"Hi, Darcy," Keisha said. The girls introduced their grandparents to each other. Grandma smiled in the vague way she had lately. Even though she was confused when she met new people, her own natural graciousness always shone through. She had always been a warm, welcoming person, and now she rose to the occasion.

"So nice to meet you," she said to Keisha's grandfather.

When Keisha and her grandfather moved on, Grandma said, "What nice people. We must have them over for dinner soon. I'll make sweet-potato pie. I made one yesterday, and Mama said it was as good as hers."

They stayed in the park until the air turned chilly, and then Darcy pushed the wheelchair home. When she neared her building, she saw her father's silver Toyota parked outside.

As Darcy wheeled Grandma towards the elevator, Dad got out of the car. He had not seen his mother-in-law since he came back, and now he stood there looking even more bewildered than Grandma. The last he had seen of Grandma, more than five years ago, she had been full of energy. Now she sat frail and shrunken in the wheelchair. He had probably kept the memory of the feisty little woman with the twinkling brown eyes, and now that image was surely shattered by reality.

"Grandma," Darcy said softly, "Dad is here."

Five years ago, Grandma was quite aware that Dad had left. She had called him many choice words over the years. Grandma could cuss someone out with the best of them. But after her stroke last year, the memory of his abandonment had blurred. Most of the time, Grandma thought Carl Wills was away on a business trip. "Hello, Carl," she said, staring at the big, burly figure before her. "I'm glad you're home."

Darcy's father reached down, took Grandma's hand, and kissed it. "It's good to see you too, Annie." He always called his mother-in-law "Annie." And during the first eleven years of the marriage, Grandma and Dad had a wonderful relationship.

"How are you, Carl? Is everything all right at work?" Grandma asked.

"Just like syrup on hotcakes, Annie," Dad replied with a warm laugh.

Grandma turned and looked at Darcy. "Well, Angelcake, what a nice surprise. Your Daddy is home early. My word, what a treat."

Darcy stood there, gripped by sadness over all that used to be and never would be again. Her father saw the look in her eyes and reached and pulled her against him. Darcy left some tears on his shoulder before they separated.

"Daddy, I'm glad you've come back," she sniffed.

"And I'm glad to know that." Dad smiled at her, his eyes wet with tears.

Chapter 10

Hakeem Randall blew away all the competition in the talent show and walked away with the grand prize—a trophy. Darcy did not even try to be among the first to congratulate him. Kids swarmed around him so thickly that he looked like a celebrity. There was even a local newspaper reporter there to interview him.

Darcy told herself that it was not Hakeem's fault that her heart raced so far ahead of his. Darcy did not share her hurt with anybody, not even Tarah. She just finished her science work in the library and walked home. On the way, she thought about calling Brisana for a trip to the mall—since Mom did not have to work today, and Darcy had a whole afternoon with nothing to do. But when she turned onto her block, she saw her father's

Toyota in front of the apartment. As Darcy got near, Jamee leaned out of the car's front window. "Dad wants to show us something, Darcy. Mom said it was okay."

Darcy got in the car, and they drove a few blocks, stopping at a pale yellow stucco house with a red tile roof. Vines with brilliant red leaves covered a trellis in the front yard.

"Cool house. You know somebody who lives here?" Jamee said.

"No, not personally. But I do know the owners are renting it with an option to buy," Dad explained. "It has three bedrooms and a den that could be made into a bedroom. Two bathrooms . . ."

"Are you talking about what I think you're talking about?" Jamee asked excitedly.

Dad smiled carefully. "I'm hoping, I'm hoping," he said.

"Can we look inside?" Jamee asked.

"Yeah, come on. The real estate lady gave me the key," Dad said, leading the way to the solid front door. The house was old, but it was in good condition. You could see that whoever lived here loved the house and took care of it.

Darcy followed Jamee down the hallway to the back bedroom. A large window looked out into the backyard where there was a little stone fountain with stone elves perched around it. "Ohhhh, Grandma would love this," Jamee sighed.

"It's only a dream right now, princess," Dad said. "Maybe a pipe dream. I'm going to talk to your Mom, and we'll see."

"Darcy," Jamee called moments later, "come look at the bathroom. It's shining, and it's got pink tile!"

"Could we afford it?" Darcy asked her father as they stood in the front hallway, ready to leave.

"Yes. It wouldn't cost much more than you're paying now for the apartment. I'm doing so well at work they'd let me sign for it," Dad said.

"We could still go to Bluford, right?" Jamee asked.

"Sure," Dad said. He got real quiet then. Finally, he said, "You know what the prettiest sight in the whole world is? It's a house at night with the windows all lit up and sounds of family. Kids laughing, music, just folks talking. A family there, you know. When I was alone in New York, I'd pass houses at night, and look into the windows, those little squares of warm light. Just looking at them and knowing a family was inside, I would think of what I'd done and what I'd ruined. I about died of shame. Guess you can say that now I'm hoping to make up for lost time."

After Dad locked the house, they stopped for ice cream. On the way home, everybody was very quiet. It was as if they were close to something wonderful and fragile—something so delicate that even the sound of their voices could damage it, make it disappear. When Dad dropped the girls off, they let themselves into the apartment without saying a word.

Saturday afternoon, the weather was so nice that Darcy took Grandma to the park again. Darcy was sitting on the stone bench reading a short story for English when a familiar voice said, "Hi. I called your house and Jamee told me you'd come down here."

"Oh. Hi," Darcy said, beaming. "Grandma, this is Hakeem from school."

"Hello," Hakeem said, gently taking Grandma's small wrinkled hand in his strong hand.

"So nice to meet you," Grandma said.

"What are you doing tomorrow, Darcy?" Hakeem asked.

"Nothing. I have to be home," Darcy answered. "Mom has a lot of stuff to do, and then she has to go to work."

"So what if I rented a movie and came over with a pizza or something?"

"You'd wanna do that?" Darcy asked in surprise.

"Yeah," Hakeem said.

"I'd have to leave the movie sometimes and check on Grandma."

Hakeem smiled. "But the rest of the time you could watch the movie with me and eat some pizza, right?"

"Sure," Darcy said, smiling.

Hakeem looked at Darcy intently. "When my Dad was going though chemo, we had to work around some things too. Everybody had to pitch in. So, if you have to pop in and out of the room while the movie's on, no sweat. That's what they made the 'Stop' button for on the VCR, right?"

A smile spread so wide across Darcy's face that she could not even control it. Hakeem walked with Darcy as she pushed Grandma's wheelchair home. They rode up in the elevator and had started towards Darcy's apartment when loud, angry voices coming from the closed door stopped them. Darcy's parents were in there shouting at each other!

Darcy froze, not sure what to do. Hakeem suggested, "Let me take your grandmother down the hall. We'll go out on that little balcony and catch some air, okay?"

Grandma was dozing, so Darcy nodded. Alone, she drew closer to the apartment door. Voices came crashing through the thin wood.

"You lied and cheated, and I don't trust you!" Mom yelled.

"I admitted I done wrong, Mattie, and I swear it won't happen again. I love you and the girls. Let me make it up to you for what I did," Dad pleaded.

"Carl Wills, you are no good. No man who runs out on his family is any good. I don't want to take a chance again. I don't want to put my heart in your hands again, just so you can stomp on it any time you please. I'm too old, Carl, too old to take risks . . ." Mom's voice was breaking.

"You're not old, Mattie. You're as beautiful now as you were the first time I saw you at Lincoln High. Baby, you walked in like a queen at the prom . . ."

"Don't try to scam me with sweet talk, Carl. Don't you be trying that phony charm, you hear? It worked when I was a teenager, but it won't work now."

"Baby, I'll spend the rest of my natural life making it up to you and the girls. I swear before God, Mattie. Don't take away my last chance to be a decent man. Don't turn me away. I swear you won't ever regret giving me another chance." Dad's voice shook with emotion.

Darcy's legs grew weak as she stood at the door. She leaned against the wall. It all hung on these moments. It would happen now, she thought, or it would never happen at all.

Darcy heard her mother weeping, then loud sobs. Then they trailed off. Darcy could not see her parents through the locked door, but she knew what was happening. It was her father's big round chest that had gently muffled her mother's sobs.

Darcy turned and ran down the hall to where Hakeem waited with Grandma. Grandma was half awake now on the balcony. "I hear the birds singing," Grandma whispered.

Hakeem looked at Darcy. "Bad?" he asked her.

"I think it might be good," Darcy said.

Hakeem gave Darcy a hug that made her catch her breath. Then Darcy leaned down and kissed Grandma's cheek. "I hear the birds too, Grandma," she said. And even though there were no birds near the little balcony, Darcy did somehow hear them, throwing their voices and their hearts to an uncertain wind, flying on faith.

Like all of us, Darcy thought.

Find out what happens next at

BLUFORD HIGH

Secrets in the Shadows

Roylin Bailey is living a nightmare—and it's all his fault. It started when the new student, Korie Archer, arrived in his history class. She was the most beautiful girl he had ever seen, and unlike most people at Bluford High, she seemed to like him. But when Roylin tried to impress her, he made a terrible mistake. Now one of his friends is gone, and someone is out to destroy him. Caught in a tightening web of lies and threats, Roylin is desperate for a way out.

Turn the page for a special sneak preview. . . .

Roylin Bailey flipped on the bathroom switch and yelled, "Mom, the switch still don't work! Didn't Tuttle fix it yet? This dump is falling apart!"

"Roylin, that man don't do nothin' around here. All he wants is to go to that racetrack and bet on horses. He'd keep gamblin' even if the ceiling fell down on us! Yesterday I had to wash the baby in water I heated on the stove 'cause we don't have enough hot water to fill a teacup!" Mrs. Bailey called back. She had complained many times, but Tuttle, the building manager, was a sour-tempered little man who always had several days' stubble on his face and a greasy Dodgers cap on his head. Requests from the tenants fell on deaf ears. But with five children, Mrs. Bailey had few choices of where to live in this neighborhood.

Roylin was almost seventeen, and he had a pretty good job as a waiter at the Golden Grill restaurant. He worked three days a week and could bring home decent money in tips, especially on Saturday nights. But most of his earnings went to pay for insurance on his mother's Honda. Because he paid for the insurance, his mother allowed him to drive the car to work and school. Between gas, insurance, and clothes, there was no way Roylin could afford to help his mother pay for a better place to live.

"Man, this place ain't fit for the roaches on the walls," Roylin yelled, kicking the bathroom door shut.

"Don't take it out on us," said Amberlynn, Roylin's fourteen-year-old sister.

"Shut your mouth!" he snapped from behind the closed door.

"Don't talk to me like that," Amberlynn yelled back. "I need a ride to school this morning," she added. "Can you take me?"

"No!"

"Mom, Roylin won't drive me to school!" Amberlynn whined.

"It's outta my way. Take the bus or walk," Roylin snapped, stepping out of the bathroom.

"What's your problem?" Amberlynn said. "You're just like Dad—mean and ugly."

Roylin turned sharply and glared at his sister. "Don't you *ever* say I'm like him! You hear me? I'm nothin' like him, nothin'!" Roylin's father used to beat him regularly, using a heavy leather strap to turn Roylin's back into a mass of tender bruises. The slightest offense was enough to enrage the muscular man. He would stand Roylin against the wall and administer blow after blow. That was why Roylin's mother finally divorced him. Even being alone with five children was not as frightening to her as living with a man whose wrath was dangerous and unpredictable. Nobody ever knew whose turn it would be to be beaten. Would he use the strap on Roylin, would he crack Amberlynn across her face, splitting her lip, or would he shove his wife so hard against the sink that she would ache for days?

"Drive your sister," Mom said crossly. "You can do that much, Roylin Bailey. It's startin' to rain, and it's a long walk to the middle school, and the bus is runnin' late as usual."

Roylin hiked his backpack onto his

shoulders. "Hurry up if you're comin' with me, Amberlynn. I don't wanna be late for my first class and get locked out."

Amberlynn stuffed one more book into her backpack and ran after her brother as he headed for his Honda. Once inside the car, Amberlynn said, "I made it onto the cheerleading squad, me and Jamee Wills. Granelli's Paint Store is paying for the uniforms. They're so nice! I'll be so good at cheering that when I get to Bluford next year I can be on the cheerleading squad there."

"Like I care," Roylin muttered.

"Hey, ain't that Bobby Wallace, that wannabe thug who was hangin' out with Londell James when you got shot?" Amberlynn asked. "How come he ain't in jail or something?"

"That punk copped a plea, and now he's back in school. They got Londell for that drive-by, though. He's the one who pulled the trigger," Roylin said, remembering the day in the park when he was shot. The memory of it still made him tremble.

Roylin pulled up at the middle school and said, "Get goin', girl. I gotta make it to Bluford before the first bell, or it's my neck. Eckerly is the meanest teacher in Bluford, and she'd just love to mess me up."

Amberlynn rushed out of the car, and Roylin drove on to Bluford High School. Steering the teal-blue Honda through the morning drizzle, he pulled into the parking lot, bolted from the car, and sprinted into the school, careful to avoid the shallow puddles that had formed on the cracked asphalt.

"Hey man," Cooper Hodden laughed as Roylin skidded into the classroom, "you always tryin' to get in under the wire. Why don't you just get up a little earlier, man?"

Roylin ignored the comment. He was sitting down when he saw a new girl sitting a desk away. She was the most beautiful girl Roylin had ever seen, even in his dreams. Her skin looked like satin, and she had huge dark eyes shadowed by long lashes. Her slightly pouting lips were smooth, full, and red.

"Man," Roylin whistled softly, "who is *that?*"

Tarah Carson sat behind Roylin. "Fool," she whispered to Roylin, "don't even *think* about that girl. Her name is Korie Archer, and she thinks she is *all that!*"

Roylin paid no attention to Ms. Eckerly's lecture on Civil War battles. He kept staring at Korie, at the way she tilted her head when she was puzzled, at how her smooth hand rubbed her neck when she grew tired of looking at the chalkboard. Roylin had dated other girls, and some of them were pretty, but no girl he had ever seen measured up to Korie. She was somebody he expected to see on the cover of a magazine, not sitting in his classroom. She had one of those incredible faces and bodies that do not seem to belong in the real world, especially the world Roylin Bailey lived in.

Roylin watched Korie glide from the room when class ended. Her perfect figure swayed through the crowd of students in the hallway. He jostled past several others to catch up to her. "Hi," he said nervously. "I'm Roylin Bailey. Today's your first day here, huh?"

Korie turned and flashed a big smile. "Yeah, I'm Korie Archer. I'm a transfer from Hoover. Do you like it here?"

"Yeah, I mean, it's okay. I'll show you around. What's your next class?"

Korie hesitated for a minute and then dug in her overcrowded purse. "I don't even know. I am so confused . . . Let's see, where's my schedule?" A lipstick and small compact fell from her purse as she rummaged around, and Roylin dove to the floor to recover them for her. When Roylin returned them, her hand brushed his, and electricity seemed to pulsate through his body. "Oh, here's the schedule. I got science next."

"I'll show you where it is," Roylin volunteered as they walked on.

"Thanks," Korie said in a musical, breathy voice.

"You got biology with Reed. She's tough. There's Room 112, right there." Roylin pointed to an open door with students streaming in.

"Well, thanks a lot, Roylin. You've been really sweet," Korie said, smiling. How could Tarah have said Korie thought she was hot stuff? She seemed as nice as she was beautiful.

"Uh . . . Korie, you and I are both in the same lunch period," Roylin said, studying her schedule carefully. "I can meet you after your algebra class, and we can go to lunch together, okay? If the rain stops, we can even go outside and eat under the trees."

"Oh, that'd be great 'cause I don't know anybody here, and I hate eating alone. You're a really nice guy, Roylin. I'm so glad I ran into you," Korie said.

"I'll meet you outside your classroom, and we'll go over to the cafeteria together," Roylin babbled on, his words tumbling over one another. "And I'll show you what's good to eat, too, 'cause some of the food here is nasty."

"Thanks," Korie said, as she headed toward class. She paused at the door and gave Roylin a little wave before disappearing into the lab classroom.

This can't be real, Roylin thought. He must be asleep in his run-down apartment having an incredible dream about a fantasy girl who actually treated him like a winner instead of the loser he really was. A guy like Hakeem Randall who could sing and play the guitar—who could make students cheer because they liked and respected him—that is the kind of guy a girl like Korie would date. Nice, pretty girls like Korie never had anything to do with the Roylins of the world. Roylin was the kind of guy girls made fun of when they gossiped about boys.

Sure, it was partly his own fault. Sometimes he taunted kids so they would feel as bad as he did. He was often rude too, but he never wanted to hurt people the way his father did. He remembered hating how his father acted, and yet he often found himself doing the same kinds of things, like he was following a script his father had written for him. Sometimes he felt trapped inside his own skin. But recently things seemed to be changing.

Since the day Roylin was grazed by a bullet at Tarah's party, people had been treating him differently. Several times over the past month, Cooper Hodden threw an arm around Roylin's shoulders and called him, "Roylin, my man." Even Hakeem invited him to join the Bluford Park Crew, a group of students who worked to keep a nearby park free from beer bottles, graffiti, and trash.

It was hard to be mean when everyone was being so nice, but Roylin knew better than to trust what was happening. He figured Cooper and Hakeem felt sorry for him, that being nice to him was just a form of charity.

But Korie was different. If she liked him, maybe things really would change. Roylin felt as if his morning classes would never end. All he could think about was having lunch with Korie.

When the bell finally rang, Roylin leaped from his desk and raced to the lab class-room so he could meet Korie.

"Hey, Roylin," Hakeem called. "Wanna study algebra with me at lunch? The quiz is coming up, and you said you wanted to work together."

"No, not today. I'm busy, real busy," Roylin said, rushing past Hakeem. As he neared the science room, he noticed Korie had already come out and was talking to Steve Morris, a varsity run-ning back for the Bluford Buccaneers.

"No, no, no," Roylin muttered to him-self, "get away from her, man. I'll bust your head! I seen her first. Don't you move in on her now!"

Roylin came up to Korie, turned his back to Steve, and said, "Let's go, Korie. We want to get in the front of the line at the cafeteria."

"Hi, Roylin. Steve was just telling me about the Bluford Buccaneers and how good you guys were this year . . ." Korie said.

"I played with the Buccaneers too," Roylin said, omitting the fact that he was a mediocre player who quit so he could work more hours. "Come on, Korie. Let's go."

"'Bye, Steve," Korie sang out as she

fell in step beside Roylin. "Everybody is so nice here. I love Bluford already, and this is only my first day!"

Roylin cast a nervous glance at the girl who, miraculously, was walking with *him*. The vultures were circling. Guys like Steve were ready to pounce on every pretty girl. But not Korie, Roylin thought. Korie belonged to him.

WELCOME TO BLUFORD HIGH

It's Not Just School—
It's Real Life

BLUFORD HIGH

The Bully
PAUL LANGAN

A new school. A new
bully. That's what
Darrell faces when
he and his mom move
from Philadelphia
to California. But
Darrell's lived in
fear long enough,
and now he must
decide whether to
run—or fight back.

Watch for these new BLUFORD HIGH titles — coming so

Until We Meet Again

Blood Is Thicker

Brothers in Arms

Summer of Secrets

■▲SCHOLASTIC
www.scholastic.com

BLF